P9-DCS-149

Hi, I'm JIMMY!

Like me, you probably noticed the world is run by adults.

But ask yourself: Who would do the best job

of making books that *kids* will love?

Yeah. **Kids!**

So that's how the idea of JIMMY books came to life.

We want every JIMMY book to be so good

that when you're finished, you'll say,

"PLEASE GIVE ME ANOTHER BOOK!"

Give this one a try and see if you agree.

(If not, you're probably an adult!)

JIMMY PATTERSON BOOKS FOR YOUNG READERS

James Patterson Presents

Ernestine, Catastrophe Queen by Merrill Wyatt

How to Be a Supervillain by Michael Fry

How to Be a Supervillain: Born to Be Good by Michael Fry

How to Be a Supervillain: Bad Guys Finish First by Michael Fry

The Unflushables by Ron Bates

Sci-Fi Junior High by John Martin and Scott Seegert

Sci-Fi Junior High: Crash Landing by John Martin and Scott Seegert

Scouts by Shannon Greenland

The Middle School Series by James Patterson

Middle School, The Worst Years of My Life

Middle School: Get Me Out of Here!

Middle School: Big Fat Liar

Middle School: How I Survived Bullies, Broccoli, and Snake Hill

Middle School: Ultimate Showdown

Middle School: Save Rafe!

Middle School: Just My Rotten Luck

Middle School: Dog's Best Friend

Middle School: Escape to Australia

Middle School: From Hero to Zero

Middle School: Born to Rock

Middle School: All Stars

The I Funny Series by James Patterson

I Funny

I Even Funnier

I Totally Funniest

I Funny TV

I Funny: School of Laughs

The Nerdiest, Wimpiest, Dorkiest I Funny Ever

The Treasure Hunters Series by James Patterson

Treasure Hunters

Treasure Hunters: Danger Down the Nile

Treasure Hunters: Secret of the Forbidden City

Treasure Hunters: Peril at the Top of the World
Treasure Hunters: Quest for the City of Gold
Treasure Hunters: All-American Adventure

The House of Robots Series by James Patterson

House of Robots
House of Robots: Robots Go Wild!
House of Robots: Robot Revolution

The Daniel X Series by James Patterson

The Dangerous Days of Daniel X
Daniel X: Watch the Skies
Daniel X: Demons and Druids
Daniel X: Game Over
Daniel X: Armageddon
Daniel X: Lights Out

Other Illustrated Novels and Stories

Ali Cross
Max Einstein: The Genius Experiment
Max Einstein: Rebels with a Cause
Dog Diaries
Dog Diaries: Happy Howlidays
Katt vs. Dogg
Unbelievably Boring Bart
Not So Normal Norbert
Laugh Out Loud
Pottymouth and Stoopid
Jacky Ha-Ha
Jacky Ha-Ha: My Life Is a Joke
Public School Superhero
Word of Mouse
Give Please a Chance
Give Thank You a Try
Big Words for Little Geniuses
Cuddly Critters for Little Geniuses
Bigger Words for Little Geniuses
The Candies Save Christmas

For exclusives, trailers, and other information, visit jimmypatterson.org.

JAMES PATTERSON BOOKS FOR YOUNG READERS AWARDS AND NOMINATIONS

THE MIDDLE SCHOOL SERIES

A Young Adult Library Services Association Quick Pick for Reluctant Young Adult Readers
A Children's Choice Book Award Nominee for Author of the Year
A #1 *New York Times* Bestseller
A #1 Indiebound Bestseller
A Nēnē Hawaii Children's Choice Award Winner
An Association for Library Service to Children Summer Reading List Book
A Delaware Diamonds Book Award Winner
An Oregon Children's Choice Award Winner
An Oregon Reader's Choice Award Nominee
A Wisconsin Golden Archer Award Nominee
A Pacific Northwest Young Reader's Choice Award Nominee
A Wyoming Soaring Eagle Book Award Nominee

THE I FUNNY SERIES

A #1 *New York Times* Bestseller
A Maryland Black-Eyed Susan Book Award Winner
A Dorothy Canfield Fisher Award Nominee
A Colorado Children's Choice Award Nominee

THE JACKY HA-HA SERIES

A #1 *New York Times* Bestseller
A Parents' Choice Award Winner
A National Parenting Products Award Winner

THE TREASURE HUNTERS SERIES

A #1 *New York Times* Bestseller

THE HOUSE OF ROBOTS SERIES

A #1 *New York Times* Bestseller

THE DANIEL X SERIES

A #1 *New York Times* Bestseller
A Louisiana Young Readers Choice Award Nominee
A Florida Sunshine State Young Readers' Award Nominee

WORD OF MOUSE

A Young Hoosier Award Nominee
A New York State Reading Association Charlotte Award Nominee
A Louisiana Young Readers' Choice Award Nominee

REBELS WITH A CAUSE

JAMES PATTERSON
AND CHRiS GRABENSTEiN
Illustrated by Beverly Johnson

JIMMY PATTERSON BOOKS
LITTLE, BROWN AND COMPANY
New York Boston London

The characters and events in this book are fictitious. Any similarity to real persons, living or dead, is coincidental and not intended by the author.

JIMMY Patterson Books / Little, Brown and Company
Hachette Book Group
1290 Avenue of the Americas, New York, NY 10104
JimmyPatterson.org

First Edition: September 2019

JIMMY Patterson Books is an imprint of Little, Brown and Company, a division of Hachette Book Group, Inc. The Little, Brown name and logo are trademarks of Hachette Book Group, Inc. The JIMMY Patterson Books® name and logo are trademarks of JBP Business, LLC.

The publisher is not responsible for websites (or their content) that are not owned by the publisher.

The Hachette Speakers Bureau provides a wide range of authors for speaking events. To find out more, go to hachettespeakersbureau.com or call (866) 376-6591.

Cataloging-in-publication data is available at the Library of Congress.

ISBN (hc) 978-0-316-48816-7, (international trade paperback) 978-0-316-45841-2

10 9 8 7 6 5 4 3 2 1

LSC-H

Printed in the United States of America

MAX EINSTEIN

REBELS WITH A CAUSE

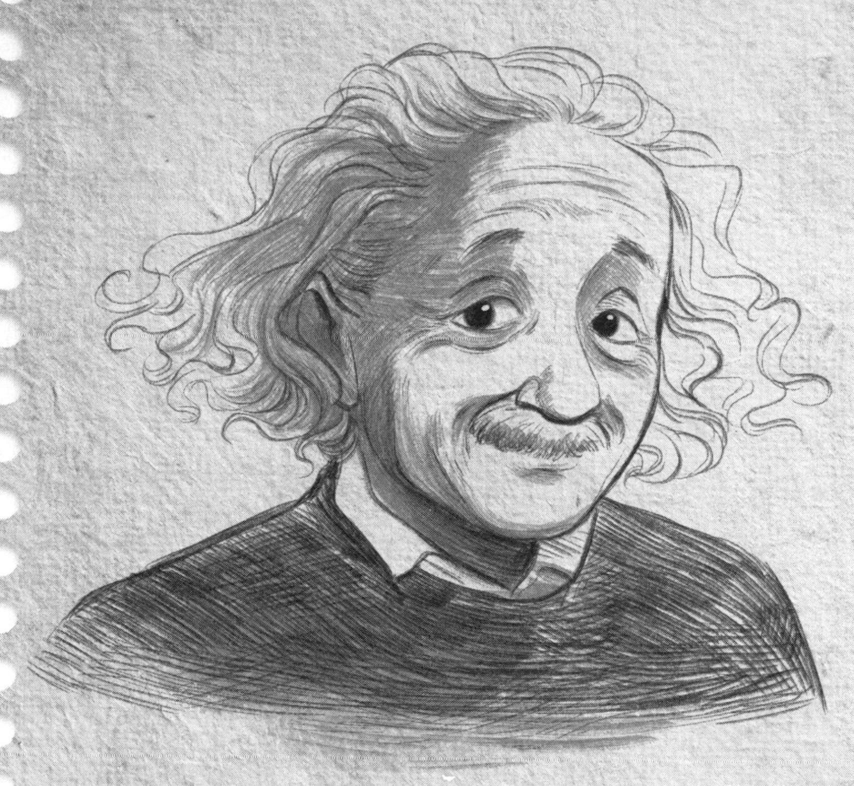

"The world is more threatened by those who tolerate evil or support it than by the evildoers themselves."

– Albert Einstein

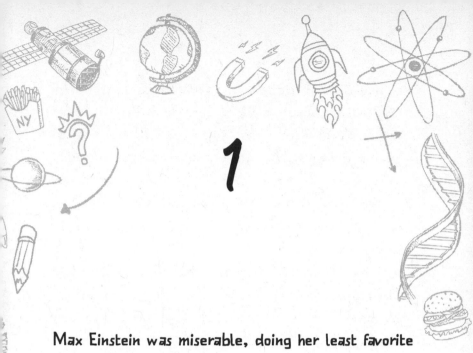

1

Max Einstein was miserable, doing her least favorite thing in the world: NOTHING!

The world's not gonna save itself! she thought.

Yes, she knew there were dangers lurking around every corner, especially after her successful adventure in Africa. But she was tired of following orders. Of "lying low" and "playing it safe." She had to get out of the room that was starting to feel more and more like a prison—complete with guards, who were stationed in the room across the hall, trying their best to disappear, which was extremely hard to do when you were a pair of six-foot-tall bodybuilders in tight-fitting suits.

Okay, to be fair, they were Max's bodyguards, there to protect her from the Corp—a dangerous group of evildoers

that would do anything to get their hands on who they considered the smartest girl in the world. But still. Max hadn't asked for them. They were Ben's idea. Ben worried a lot, especially for a fourteen-year-old billionaire. (Yeah.)

Max checked the weather app on her smartphone. Ninety-two degrees with 90 percent humidity. Sweltering. New York City could become a steamy concrete sauna in the summer.

"I need to be outside," she told the Einstein bobblehead doll smiling at her from inside the battered old suitcase she'd propped open in the corner of her small dormitory room. It was Max's portable shrine to all things Einstein. She used to have a very nice, brand-new apartment over a renovated horse stable. But a few months ago, Ben had insisted that Max move somewhere safer and more "secure" where she could spend most of her time doing what she was doing this weekend.

NOTHING!

A body at rest tends to stay at rest, she told herself, remembering Sir Isaac Newton's first law of motion. *A body in motion will remain in motion.*

It was time to get her body moving.

Max pulled her curly mop of copper-colored hair into a ponytail. Slipping a bathrobe over her shorts and T-shirt (which had *Star Wars* lettering spelling out "May the Mass

The Scientific Method for Sneaking Out.

Clueless bodyguards.
Mirror positioning critical because the angle at which the light ray approaches the mirror surface is equal to the angle at which it departs from the mirror surface.
Outdoor clothing carefully concealed.

Times Acceleration Be with You"), she slid into a pair of rubbery flip-flops. She tucked her sneakers and socks into a shower tote, hiding them underneath the shampoo and loofah sponge. She also slid in a small hand mirror.

Max stepped into the hallway outside Room 723 and headed up the corridor.

The two bodyguards, both men, stepped out of the room across the hall. They wore matching curly-wire earpieces.

"Hi, guys," said Max. "Just going to grab a quick shower."

The two men nodded. "Be, uh, safe," said the one named Jamal.

"We'll be here if, you know, you need anything," said the younger one, whose name was Danny.

Neither one of them wanted to be anywhere near the girls' communal bathrooms in a college dormitory. Yes, Max was only twelve, but she was at Columbia University. Not as a student. She was what they called an "adjunct professor." That meant, during the week, she *taught* college kids.

"Thanks, guys," Max said to her two bodyguards.

She ambled up the hall as casually as she could. The showers were located just past Room 716.

So were the exit stairs.

She glanced down at the hand mirror that she had positioned so she could see what was happening behind her.

When she walked past the staircase door and made the right turn into the bathroom, both men disappeared back into Room 722. Max flushed the toilet, just to give them something watery to listen to. Then, she hung up her bathrobe, sat down on the commode, lost the flip-flops, and changed into her walking shoes.

She snuck one more rearview-mirror glance up the hallway.

The coast was clear.

She'd come back for the shower tote later. She might even take a shower.

But first she had to bust out of "prison" and go DO something...anything!

On her own.

With no protection.

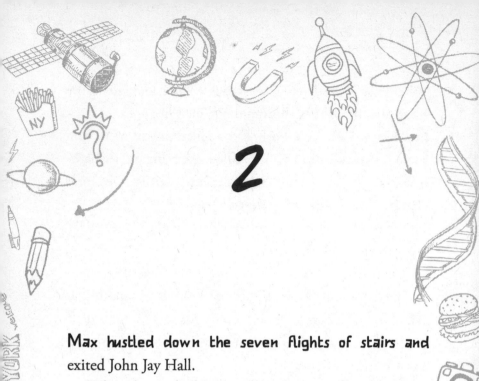

2

Max hustled down the seven flights of stairs and exited John Jay Hall.

When she reached Amsterdam Avenue and 114th Street, she started heading north at a brisk pace, her radar up. She wasn't being followed.

At 120th Street, she pulled out her secure phone (another "gift" from Ben) and tapped the speed dial number for Charl and Isabl, the highly skilled tactical team that headed up security for the Change Makers Institute, where Max was considered "The Chosen One."

That title always made Max roll her eyes.

"The Chosen One."

It sounded so . . . so . . . *Harry Potter.*

But Ben, the super-rich benefactor, had selected Max to

head up his team of elite young geniuses, all of whom were charged with making the world a better place.

Yeah.

Ben was an ambitious young guy with big dreams and an even bigger budget. "We aim to make significant changes to save this planet and the humans who inhabit it," Max had been told when she visited the CMI headquarters in Jerusalem. And Ben only trusted kids to help him do it.

"Max?" Charl answered. He had an interesting accent that Max still couldn't quite place. Israeli? Eastern European? Basically, it was mysterious and foreign. "Where are you?"

"Out."

"What? Are Jamal and Danny with you?"

"No. But it's not their fault. They think I'm in the shower."

Charl sighed. "Max, we talked about this. You need security. The Corp has spies everywhere...."

The Corp. The evil empire out to stop the CMI. Where Ben and the CMI wanted to make changes and improve the human condition, the Corp wanted to make money and improve the bottom line in its bank accounts. One member, Dr. Zacchaeus Zimm, also wanted to lure Max away. He was like the Corp's Darth Vader, always trying to tempt Max to join the dark side of the Force.

So far, it wasn't working.

So far.

But Dr. Zimm had hinted that he knew something about Max's past. He might even know who her parents were and why she was named "Max Einstein." Max couldn't remember her parents. She'd lived in orphanages, foster care facilities, and with other homeless people her whole life. Until, of course, the CMI came along and flew her off to Jerusalem.

"Max?" Charl's voice was strong and firm over the phone. "Your job, right now, is to stay safe. Dr. Zimm and the Corp are still after you. Please return to your dormitory. Immediately."

"When's our next mission?" asked Max, basically ignoring Charl. She was a lot like her idol, Dr. Einstein. She didn't do well with authority or direct orders.

"There will be no 'next mission' for the CMI if Dr. Zimm grabs you, Max."

"Fine," she said. "Then I'll have to find my own."

"Max?"

"Just obeying Sir Newton's first law, Charl. I'm a body in motion. I need to keep moving."

She disconnected the call and powered down her phone so Charl couldn't call back.

When she reached Martin Luther King Boulevard, she turned right and headed into Harlem.

As the boulevard angled into West 125th Street, Max

saw a group of happy kids outside a bodega. They were jumping through the sideways stream of water gushing out of an open fire hydrant, trying to cool down.

"Hey, you kids!" shouted an angry old man on a stoop. He had a towel wrapped around his waist. "I'm trying to take a shower upstairs! You're making the water pressure drop!"

The kids just laughed and splashed some more.

"That does it! I'm calling the cops."

The old man shook his fist and headed inside, no doubt to pick up a phone and punch in 911.

Max sprang into action. She had to. She couldn't lie low or play it safe. Not when a bunch of kids were about to get into trouble for just being kids.

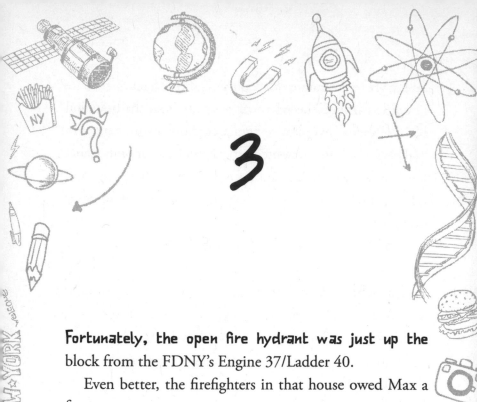

3

Fortunately, the open fire hydrant was just up the block from the FDNY's Engine 37/Ladder 40.

Even better, the firefighters in that house owed Max a favor.

About two months ago, right after she first moved to the Columbia dorm, she was able to help Engine 37 on a call to a burning building. They were having trouble assessing the situation on the upper floors, because their brand-new drone—which carried both a high-def *and* an infrared camera—wouldn't lift off. The drone's cameras were supposed to let the chief at the street-level command post see where the firefighters were on the roof and what the fire was up to behind the walls.

But the drone wouldn't fly.

So Max gave him a quick flying-camera hack.

"Take the cameras off the drone," she told the battalion chief. "Find a clear plastic garbage bag and a wire hanger to make a rig for the cameras. Grab a can of Sterno out of that grocery store, light it, secure it to the coat-hanger rig, and we can make a rudimentary hot air balloon to float your cameras up to the roof."

The battalion chief, whose badge ID'd him as Morkal, stared at her.

Max held his gaze.

"You heard the girl," Chief Morkal barked. "Make me a hot air balloon out of a garbage bag! Stat!"

"Just make sure it's all clear, sir," reminded Max. "Otherwise..."

"Right. All we're gonna see is a black screen."

The firefighters rigged up the mini-blimp and sent the two cameras up to do their job.

Now Max hoped she could ask these same firefighters to help the neighborhood kids who, in their attempt to cool off, had broken the law by wrenching open a fire hydrant.

She burst into the firehouse and saw a familiar face.

"Chief Morkal?"

"Oh, hey, Max. How's it going?"

"Not bad, sir, but, well, I need your help."

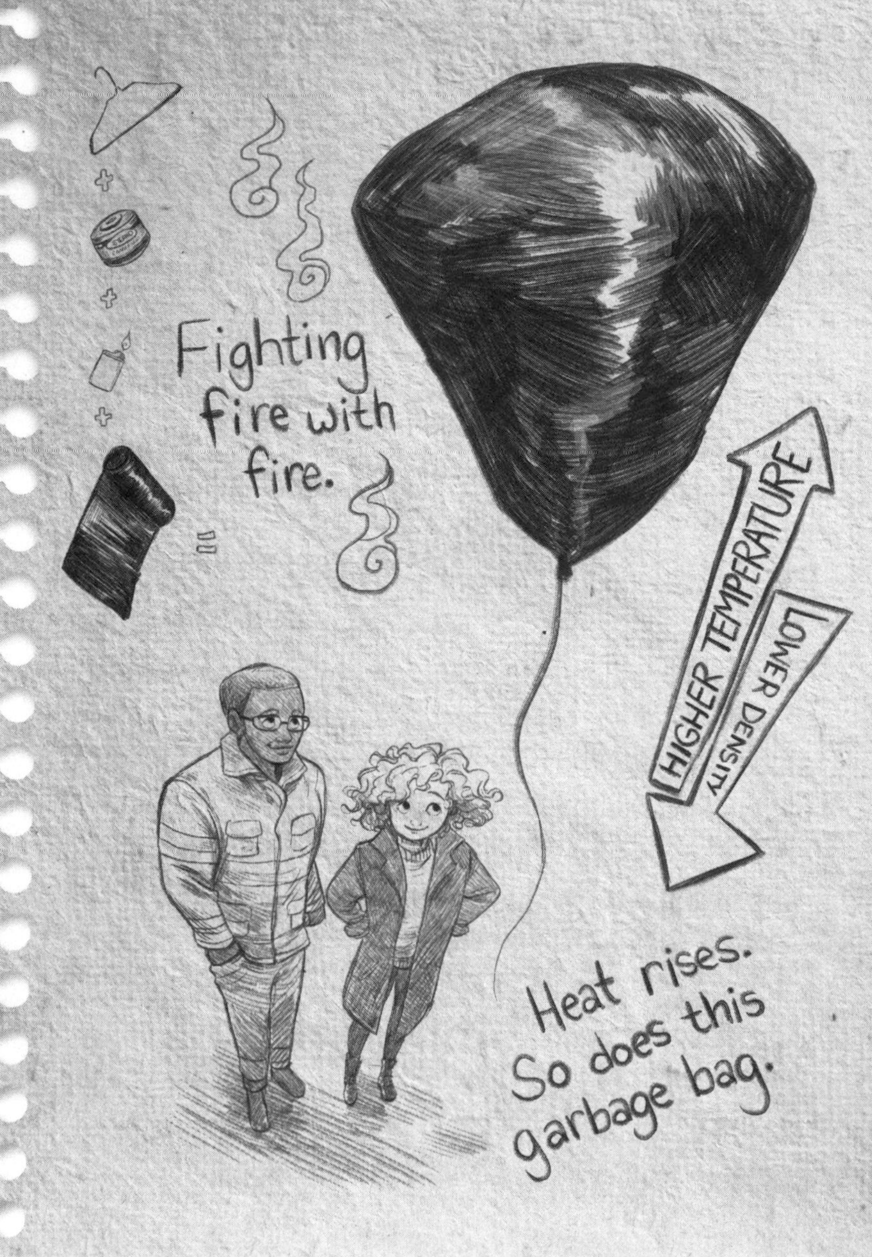
Fighting fire with fire.
HIGHER TEMPERATURE
LOWER DENSITY
Heat rises. So does this garbage bag.

"You want to make a bigger balloon?" cracked Chief Morkal. "Maybe enter it in the Macy's parade?"

"No, sir. I mean, that would be fun... but, right now, we have a fire hydrant situation."

"Where?"

"Up the street. It needs a sprinkler cap."

"Not a problem."

"Except it needs it right now. Otherwise, a bunch of kids could wind up in trouble. NYC municipal code says the penalty is thirty days in jail or a thousand-dollar fine."

"They opened the hydrant?"

Max nodded.

"Let me go grab some tools," said the battalion chief.

"You're going to do it yourself?"

"Hey, I owe you, Max. Plus, it's so hot, I might join the kids jumpin' through the water!"

Max and the chief marched up the street with a spray cap—a clever device that turned the gush of water jetting out of a hydrant into a sprinkler. The nozzle would limit the amount of water exploding out of the open hydrant from one thousand gallons per minute to about twenty-five.

"Won't sting so much, either," Chief Morkal told the kids when the cap was safely installed and spraying out water in a cluster of gentle, arcing streams.

The kids were happy.

The old man who'd wanted to take a shower was happy, too. In fact, he came back outside in his swimsuit so he could jump through the gurgling water with his young neighbors.

The police were thrilled that the situation had "cooled down" before they arrived.

Max believed that for every problem there was a solution.

You just had to find it and then do the hard work to make it happen.

4

With the hydrant problem solved, Max was feeling giddy.

She was *free, free, free.* No dorm room. No bodyguards. No Ben or Charl or Isabl telling her what she should be doing.

She started riffing on old-school song titles. (For reasons beyond comprehension, even for an Einstein, Max *loved* classic rock.)

Free Bird! Free Ride! I'm Free! People Got to Be Free! Rockin' in the Free World! I Want to Be Free!

Max hopped on the subway at 125th Street and St. Nicholas Avenue and headed downtown to visit an old friend. She hopped off the A train at West 4th Street—the

same stop she used when she went to NYU—and clambered up the steep steps.

Washington Square Park was only a few blocks away. She found Mr. Leonard "Lenny" Weinstock exactly where she hoped she would: at the concrete chess tables.

"Hey, Mr. Weinstock!" she called out with a wave.

"Maxine?" said Mr. Weinstock, in a British accent that Max always figured was fake, even though Mr. Weinstock claimed that he graduated from Oxford and was close personal friends with all the royals. "What are you doing downtown, Maxine?"

"I needed to get out, sir. Stretch my legs *and* my brain. You up for a game?"

"I'm not certain that would be such a good idea...."

"Why not? You're sitting at a chess table. You have all the pieces set up—"

"I was contemplating a game against myself."

"Where's the fun in that?"

"Simple, Maxine. Even when I lose, I also win."

"Come on," Max urged. "This won't take long. Last time, the game was over in three moves."

"But, Max, correct me if I'm wrong, aren't you supposed to be lying low and playing it safe?"

"I'd rather play chess. Unless, of course, you're chicken."

"Hardly." Mr. Weinstock bopped a button on top of his speed chess timer. "Game on."

Max took it easy on Mr. Weinstock. This time, she defeated him in five moves.

"Ah, the Scholar's Mate scenario," said Mr. Weinstock, admiringly. "Well played, Maxine. Well played, indeed."

"You ready to go again?"

"Max?"

"Yes?"

"Where are Jamal and Danny?"

"Probably in the girls' bathroom, wondering how I can take a shower without running any water."

"I beg your pardon?"

"Long story. I wanted to spend my free Sunday being, I don't know, *free*."

"Even though it might jeopardize your CMI team's next big project?"

"There is no next big project."

"Yes, there is. Mr. Abercrombie is fielding requests and formulating an action plan."

Mr. Abercrombie is what Mr. Weinstock called Ben. Probably because the CMI benefactor's full name was Benjamin Franklin Abercrombie and Mr. Weinstock, who was in his fifties, was more formal than most.

"You and your team did amazing things with your solar power solutions in the Congo, Maxine," Mr. Weinstock continued. "Amazing things, indeed."

"True, I guess. But the key word in your first sentence was 'did.' It's already been done. What do we do next? What do we do *now*?"

"Simple. Be patient."

"I'm not the only one eager to get going again," said Max. "I've been texting and e-mailing with everybody else on the team. They're all itching for more action. Even Klaus."

Mr. Weinstock put a finger to his lips. "Be careful, Max," he whispered. "The Corp has eyes and ears everywhere."

That startled Max. Just slightly.

"Do they know where I am?" she whispered back, her eyes darting around, scanning all the strangers in the park, looking for a familiar egg-shaped sinister face. One with sharp teeth too large for his smile. Dr. Zimm.

"No, Maxine," said Mr. Weinstock. "They do not know your current residence. However, they *do* know where you used to live."

With that, he pulled out his phone.

"I think you should watch this video clip, dear."

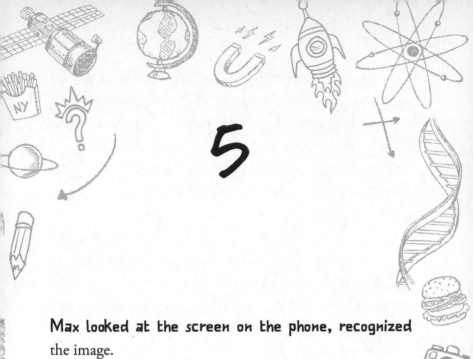

5

Max looked at the screen on the phone, recognized the image.

It was her old apartment, the one above the horse stables.

“I figured you guys had security cameras watching me,” she said.

“Indeed,” said Mr. Weinstock, tapping the Play icon. “Several of them.”

“So, why aren’t I in the picture?”

“This particular footage was recorded just yesterday. Long after you’d checked out.”

“No one’s in my old room? I left months ago. . . .”

“There have been several formerly homeless tenants since,” said Mr. Weinstock. “But, fortunately, thanks to our training initiatives and contacts in the business world,

all of them have moved on to new jobs and homes of their own. Your old room was vacant when these unannounced visitors dropped by. Ah. Here they come. Through the bathroom window."

Max studied the high-definition footage, shot from multiple camera angles. It jumped around like an action movie—from the entrance to the living room to the kitchen and back again. Two men dressed in black cargo pants, black turtlenecks, and black beanies could be seen outside the window, jimmying it open with a pry bar.

"Seriously?" said Max. "The Corp's thugs dress like cat burglars in a heist movie? Did they forget their burglar masks?"

"No, we suspect they wanted us to see their faces."

"Why?"

"So we could run them through our facial recognition software and realize that the first man into your room, the one with the tiger tattoo crawling up the back of his neck, is Friedrich Hoffman. Very ruthless. Very efficient. He also enjoys opera."

Max looked at Mr. Weinstock. He shrugged.

"We all have our hobbies, Max."

Max watched as the two men in black trashed her old room. They pulled drawers out of dressers. Flipped over the mattress. Ransacked the kitchen cupboards.

"Ah," said Mr. Weinstock, "the second gentleman, the

one so mercilessly tearing apart the cabinetry, is Mr. Pinky Mulligan."

"And what does Pinky like?" asked Max. "Irish step dancing?"

"Not particularly. However, Pinky is so named because, as you might notice if we were to zoom in a little closer on his left hand, he lost his pinky finger in a barroom brawl when he was sixteen. Both of these gentlemen have extensive arrest records. They are also known foot soldiers for the Corp and, according to our best intel, report directly to Dr. Zacchaeus Zimm."

Suddenly, the surveillance video ended.

Ben was on the screen.

"And this, Max," he said, "is why you need to stick to our plan."

Max couldn't help but grin. She did every time she saw Ben. He was kind of quirky. Kind of geeky. Kind of cute. He was also super intelligent and had a great heart, the kind that really wanted to save the world, even though, when it came to actually being *in* the world, Ben was super awkward. His social skills weren't the best. Sort of like Max's. Maybe because they both lived in their heads too much. Maybe because they'd both lost their parents at a very young age.

Actually, Max had never really known her parents.

Loss. Loneliness. They had that in common. Maybe that's why she and Ben got along so well.

"So, Max—I mean Adjunct Professor Paula Ehrenfest..."

Now Ben made Max laugh. The alias they'd created for Max's position at Columbia University (a position paid for by Ben through his Benjamin Franklin Abercrombie Foundation) was a tribute to one of Albert Einstein's physicist friends, Paul Ehrenfest.

"...you see what the Corp is capable of. Now will you please listen to me? Your next project is coming. Soon. I promise. We're fielding several requests, looking for the perfect opportunity. Right now, the most important thing you can do is to stay safe! You're my team leader."

Okay, thought Max. *If the warning comes directly from Ben, I should probably listen.*

"Fine," Max said when Ben's video clip ended. "You and Ben made your point, Mr. Weinstock. I'll head back up to Columbia on the subway."

"No need," said Mr. Weinstock, pocketing his phone. "I believe your ride just arrived."

He nudged his head to the left.

To where the sunglasses-wearing Jamal and Danny stood with their arms crossed over their chests.

And, yes, they were both wearing suits. Even though it was 95 degrees in the shade.

6

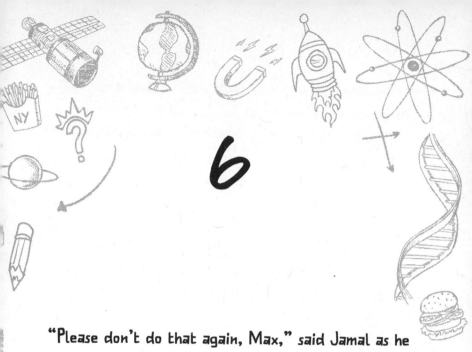

"Please don't do that again, Max," said Jamal as he piloted the black Lincoln MKZ uptown.

"You made me go into the bathroom," said Danny. "Women yelled at me, Max. My ears are still ringing."

"Your face is still kind of red, too," said Max.

"Yeah, Danny," said Jamal, and laughed. "It is. What'd they call you?"

Danny slumped down in his seat. "A pawn of the patriarchy."

"Nice," said Max.

"Look, Max," said Jamal, "this little cat-and-mouse game has been fun, but word is the Corp is on your trail."

"Yeah," said Max, gazing out the window as the car

rolled north through the canyons of Manhattan. "Ben told me."

"So, you'll play nice?" said Jamal, glancing at her in the rearview mirror.

"Yeah."

"Good. My daughter's dance recital is next weekend. Don't want to miss it because I'm chasing after you."

"But that thing with the mirror tucked into the shower tote so you could see behind you?" said Danny. "That was smart, Max. Very impressive."

"Thanks."

On Monday morning, Max (a.k.a. Adjunct Professor Paula Ehrenfest) was walking down the seventh-floor corridor of John Jay Hall, flanked by Jamal and Danny. She was off to teach her first class of the day.

"Excuse me, Paula?"

It was Nancy Hanker. The resident adviser for the seventh floor. RAs were supposed to plan community-building activities for the floor and help residents if they had any problems or issues.

They were *not* supposed to give residents the stink-eye, which was, basically, all Nancy Hanker ever did when she saw Max, Jamal, or Danny.

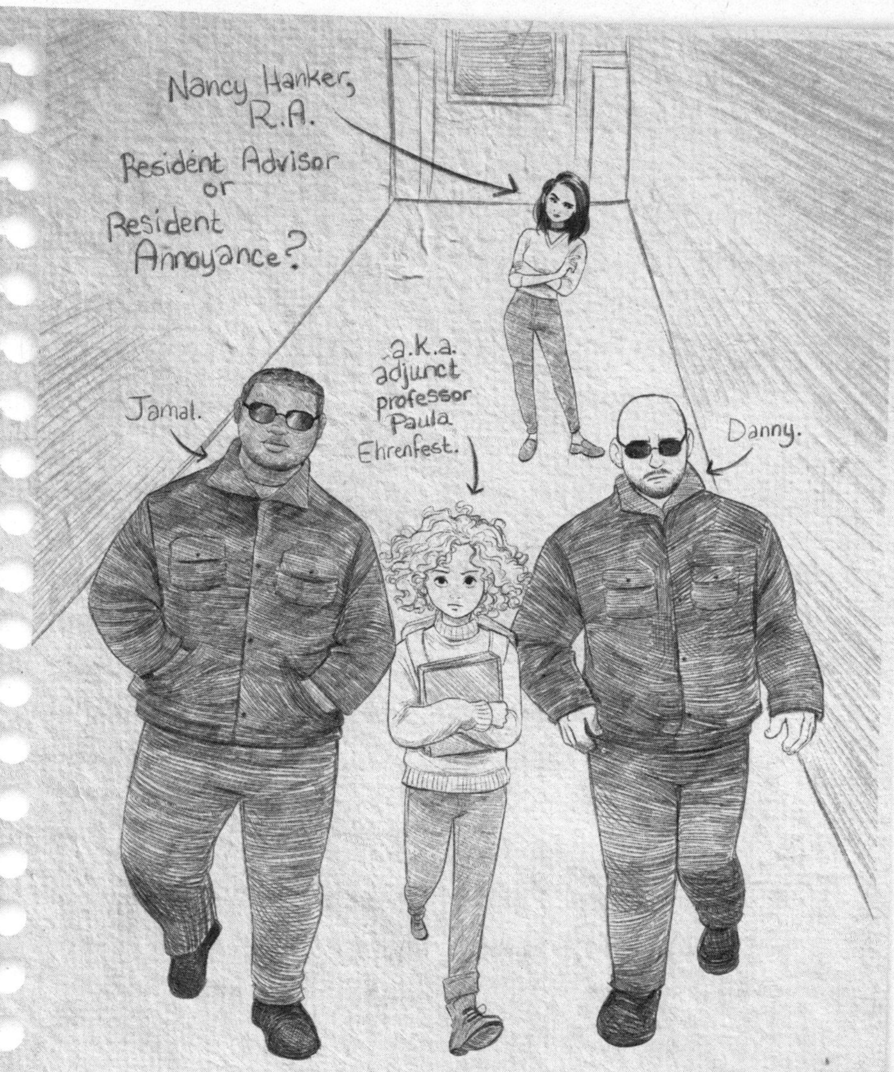
Nancy Hanker, R.A.
Resident Advisor or Resident Annoyance?
a.k.a. adjunct professor Paula Ehrenfest.
Jamal.
Danny.
They look like Secret Service agents.
They make me feel protected.

Nancy Hanker did not like the twelve-year-old physics prodigy residing on her floor. She also didn't like her bodyguards.

"Hey, Nancy," said Max. "We're kind of in a hurry. I'm lecturing about special relativity and relativistic kinematics this morning."

Nancy didn't blink. "It's about your... security team."

"Ma'am?" said Jamal, stepping forward. "Is there a problem?"

"Yes. This is a dormitory. None of the other residents have private bodyguards."

"I'm sure if the president's daughter were going to school here, she'd have Secret Service protection."

"I'll let you know if it ever happens," said Nancy. "I talked to campus security. You two gentlemen can't stay on the floor anymore."

"Excuse me, ma'am," said Danny. "We are here on—"

Nancy showed him the palm of her hand.

"I know. Some wealthy benefactor endowed the adjunct professor princess here and paid for you guys to be her private security detail. But we have a housing shortage at Columbia. We need your room. For a student! Rent a van. Sleep in it. Have a nice day."

Nancy Hanker returned to her room and slammed the door.

"This presents a problem," muttered Jamal.

"There are no problems, only solutions," Max muttered back.

"John Lennon wrote that," said Danny. "For a song."

"Yes, he did," said Max. "Come on, you guys. We can't be late for class. We'll deal with this other stuff later. That's why time was invented."

"Huh?" said Danny.

"Just something Albert Einstein said: 'The only reason there is time is so that everything doesn't happen at once.' "

7

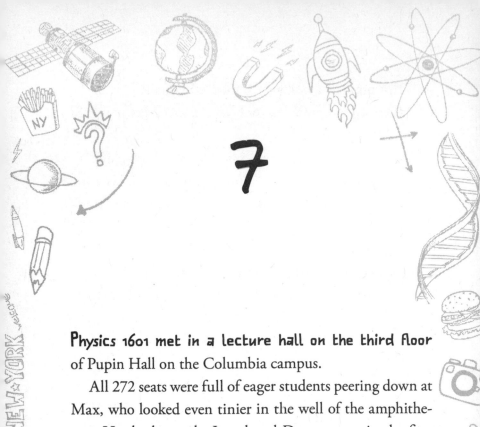

Physics 1601 met in a lecture hall on the third floor of Pupin Hall on the Columbia campus.

All 272 seats were full of eager students peering down at Max, who looked even tinier in the well of the amphitheater. Her bodyguards, Jamal and Danny, were in the first row. They did not have notebooks or pens.

"Today," Max told her audience, "I'd like to look at one of Albert Einstein's most famous thought experiments—what he called *Gedankenexperiment*—"

"Because it's German!" said a student in the front row named Johnathan Phillips (the same student who thought he should be leading the lecture instead of "some twelve-year-old nerd with frizzy hair").

Max ignored Johnathan Phillips. She often had to.

"In this thought experiment," Max continued, "Dr. Einstein was exploring the relativity of simultaneity. Whether two events occur at exactly the same time is never one hundred percent definite. It all depends on how and where you look at those two events. What's really cool about thought experiments is that you don't need a lab or equipment or even a calculator. You just need your brain and your imagination."

"Like me imagining that a twelve-year-old girl can teach me anything," Johnathan Phillips muttered snidely to the student sitting to his left.

Max ignored him. Again.

"Here's one of Einstein's most famous thought experiments." Max went to the chalkboard and started drawing a train with several cars, two cartoon Einsteins—one on the train, one on a train platform—and two lightning bolts striking either end of the platform. "Okay. We have one observer standing here, in the middle of a railroad station platform. Another observer is on a train pulling into the station. The train's traveling at nearly the speed of light. Guess it was an early bullet train."

The students in the lecture hall laughed.

"Lightning strikes either side of the train platform at the exact same second. The observer on the platform is right in the middle—the same distance from each lightning bolt."

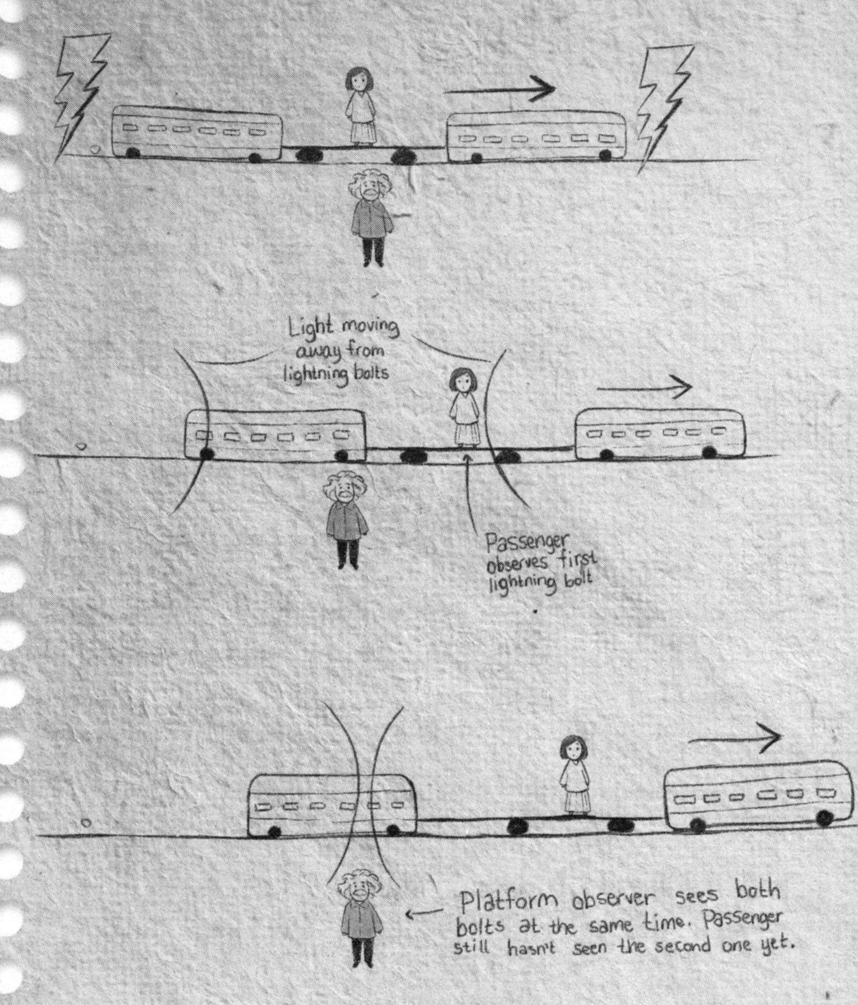

Lightning striking twice.
At the same time?
It depends from where you're looking at it.

"What does the person on the platform see?" Max asked her audience.

"Simultaneous lighting strikes," said a student in the third row.

"Okay. How about the passenger? The observer on the moving train?"

No one answered, but everyone (except maybe Johnathan Phillips) was thinking about it.

"Dr. Einstein tells us," Max continued, "that, to the observer on the moving train, events that happen in the direction the train is traveling will appear to happen *before* events behind it. Therefore, for our passenger, the lightning will hit one end of the platform, the one the train is moving toward, before it hits the end of the platform behind the train—even though the observer on the platform will swear up and down that both lightning bolts struck at exactly the same time. The whole idea of something happening simultaneously is thrown out the window when we add movement."

"I say the lightning is there and not there!" said Phillips. "Because of quantum theory!"

"Not if it has been observed, Mr. Phillips," said Max. "Which, in this thought experiment, it has been. Twice."

Phillips stood up.

"Oh, I see you've read a book or two about quantum

physics," he said, moving forward, as if to challenge Max. Jamal and Danny, her bodyguards, were, suddenly, paying very close attention to Max's lecture.

"Yes," said Max. "I am familiar with the uncertainty principle. Is the moon out tonight? The answer is yes *and* no. It is both there and not there—until I look up and see it in the night sky."

"Then why couldn't your hero, Dr. Einstein, accept that reality was this weird? Why didn't he buy into the bizarreness of quantum physics?"

"Because he was wrong. Something, I am assuming, Mr. Phillips, that you have never been. . . ."

"Ooooh," said the other 271 students. Some started pulling out their smartphones to record the confrontation gathering steam like the thunderheads creating those lightning bolts in the thought experiment.

"However," Max continued, "by trying to disprove the 'uncertainty principle' Einstein did discover 'quantum entanglement.' "

Phillips stepped forward. "Quantum entanglement? Is that what you call it when something gets stuck in your hair? And, by the way, who do I talk to about getting a refund? I'm not paying an Ivy League tuition to be lectured to by a twelve-year-old girl."

He took another step forward.

It was one too many.

Jamal and Danny were on him in a nanosecond.

And every phone in the lecture hall captured the moment Johnathan Phillips was wrestled to the floor.

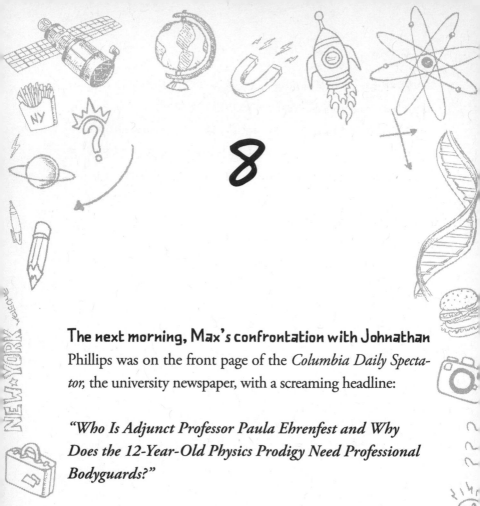

8

The next morning, Max's confrontation with Johnathan Phillips was on the front page of the *Columbia Daily Spectator,* the university newspaper, with a screaming headline:

"Who Is Adjunct Professor Paula Ehrenfest and Why Does the 12-Year-Old Physics Prodigy Need Professional Bodyguards?"

Under it was a photograph of Johnathan Phillips being thrown to the lecture hall floor by Jamal and Danny.

Phillips was clutching the rolled-up homework assignment Max had handed out when the class started. Phillips had earned an A. But since he was such a jerk, Max had

spitefully switched it to an A–. But then, after speaking to Albert Einstein, she realized that was wrong.

Max didn't actually speak to the most famous physicist in history. After all, Dr. Einstein passed away in 1955. But she did have imaginary conversations with him in her head. His voice was gentle, the way a kindly grandfather might sound (not that Max had ever had one of those, either).

"Treat Mr. Phillips the way *you* wish to be treated, Max," her Einstein voice had told her.

"But he never shows me any respect."

"And so you wish to sink to his level?"

"No. Not really."

"Good. Example isn't just another way to teach. It is the *only* way to teach."

Phillips had done the work. He deserved the proper credit. So, Max had done the only thing she could do (especially after checking in with her internal mentor). With a vertical flick of her red pen, she'd turned the spiteful A– into a glowing A+.

Ben must've seen the front-page article and picture. He sent Max an urgent text at 7:32 a.m.:

No more classes this week.

Lie low. Stay safe. I'll be in touch.

Great. She was already lying low! Now Ben wanted her to lie even lower?

Max hurried downstairs to check in with her security detail. (Thanks to Nancy Hanker, they were camping out in an RV parked on the street outside her dormitory.)

"This could blow your cover, Max," said Jamal, tapping a copy of the student paper. "You should stay indoors today."

"We may need to initiate a rapid extraction," added Danny.

"If the Corp sees that newspaper article..." said Jamal, letting that thought hang in the air.

"Yeah," said Max, understanding completely. "We may have to move again. Sorry."

"It's not your fault," said Danny. "That Phillips kid was out of line. And hey, if Albert Einstein can make a mistake or two, so can anyone."

Max went back to her room and reread some of the postcards and letters she'd received from the other members of the CMI team, all of whom were back home with their families.

Home.

Family.

Max really didn't really have either one of those. She'd only been at Columbia for two months and now, thanks to the photo in the school newspaper, she might need to move again.

She looked at the postcard Klaus had sent her from Poland. It had been mailed to her old address, the apartment over the horse stables. Klaus was a bit of a blowhard and extremely self-centered. But he was wicked smart. Especially when it came to robotics and AI—artificial intelligence.

He also thought he should be the CMI team leader instead of Max.

"Should the pressure of being the 'Chosen One' prove too much for you," Klaus had written, "please know that I am ready, willing, and able to assume that heavy burden and all its responsibilities at your earliest convenience."

Did Max think Klaus was a pompous buffoon who ate way too much sausage? Or was he just a smart kid who had such an inferiority complex that he had to constantly boast to inflate his ego? That, too, was relative. It all depended on what day you asked and what Klaus had just done—something brilliant or something bizarre.

Since Max had more or less been confined to her quarters for the rest of the day, she did what she often did when she was restless or confused or couldn't sleep: She struck up another conversation with Albert Einstein.

9

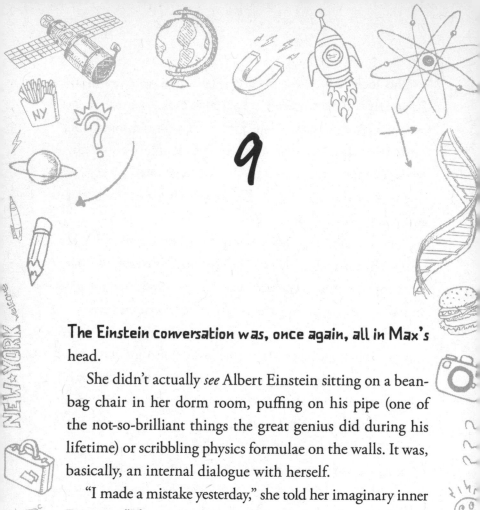

The Einstein conversation was, once again, all in Max's head.

She didn't actually *see* Albert Einstein sitting on a beanbag chair in her dorm room, puffing on his pipe (one of the not-so-brilliant things the great genius did during his lifetime) or scribbling physics formulae on the walls. It was, basically, an internal dialogue with herself.

"I made a mistake yesterday," she told her imaginary inner Einstein. "I let an annoying student push my buttons."

"Ah," her Einstein replied. "I think you're being too hard on yourself. Besides, a person who never made a mistake never tried anything new. Have you ever read about my 'cosmological constant,' a mathematical fix I created for my theory of relativity?"

"Yes," said Max. "I've, uh, studied all your, you know, goofs."

"You mean my mistakes."

"Yeah. You sort of fudged your formula...."

"And a Russian mathematician named Friedmann proved me wrong and, in so doing, developed the Big Bang Theory."

"Yeah. I read about that, too."

"So you see, Max—my error led directly to a major scientific breakthrough, not to mention an amusing sitcom on TV. Maybe your error will lead to similar positive results."

"I don't see how it could."

"I felt the same way when Friedmann did his math and showed the world how wrong I was," said her Einstein with a small chuckle. "But remember this, Max: The only sure way to avoid making mistakes is to have no new ideas."

Suddenly, there was a knock on the door.

Max called out, "Yes?"

"It's Emma from down the hall."

Max opened her door.

"Hey," she said.

"Hey," said Emma. "You're super smart, right?"

Max grinned. "That's relative..."

"Well, we have an emergency. In the study. We need your brain—and your nose!"

Max followed Emma up the corridor to the lounge, a

room with a few chairs, footstools, and a whiteboard—plus a microwave oven. It was a great place for a group to study together.

"What's that smell?" she asked.

"Somebody nuked something extremely malodorous in the microwave. The whole room reeks."

There was a group of five students huddled in the hall, all of them holding their noses.

"Does anybody have any vanilla extract?" Max asked.

"Um, this is Columbia University," said Emma. "Not my mother's kitchen."

"Right. But a drop or two of vanilla on a warm lightbulb can quickly deodorize a room." Max snapped her fingers. "Aha. Dryer sheets."

"I have a bunch of those," said Emma. "For laundry."

"Go grab them. How about a fan?"

"I have one in my room," said a girl named Madison.

"Bring it to the lounge. We'll stick some dryer sheets to the back of the fan, the side where it's drawing in air. When we turn on the fan, the sheets will be sucked up against the grille, locking them in place. As the fan blows, we'll get cool, circulating air that smells great."

Five minutes later, another problem was solved.

"Awesome!" said Emma. "We're extremely fortunate to have you on our floor, Professor!"

TIME OUT CORNER

Stress energy tensor

+ Lorentz boost in x-direction @ velocity $v = \beta c$ =

We all make mistakes, Max.
Like this hairdo.

"Ha!" said the one dissenting voice in the hallway.

Nancy Hanker, the RA.

"I saw your picture in the paper this morning," she said to Max. "I knew those bodyguards of yours were nothing but trouble. They ever do anything like that on my dorm floor and I promise: You'll be evicted from John Jay Hall faster than the speed of light squared. Do I make myself clear?"

Max just nodded.

"Good. And why does my lounge smell like fabric softener?"

Max grinned. "So my friends can study without gagging. Excuse me. I need to go work on my lecture notes."

Max was feeling pretty good as she made her way back to her room.

Not even Nancy Hanker could ruin her mood.

Because Max didn't realize who else had just read the *Columbia Daily Spectator.*

10

"She wasn't there," said Mr. Mulligan, the thug with the Irish accent.

The one who was also missing most of the pinky finger on his left hand.

"The place was empty," said his partner, Mr. Hoffman. His accent was slightly German. When he was angry, like he was now, the tiger tattooed on his neck seemed to pounce in time to his pulse.

"You gentlemen are not at fault," said their boss, a bald scientist with sharp teeth too large for his sneer. "We were operating with outdated data from an unreliable source."

They were meeting at the scientist's high-tech research facility outside of Boston.

"We know you want her bad, Dr. Zimm," said Mulligan.

"It's not just for me, gentlemen," said Dr. Zimm, rubbing his skeletal hands together. "It's for the future of Western civilization. With Max Einstein on the Corp's team, we can build better, smarter weapons that will keep the world safer and more secure. With her brain, mankind's potential will know no bounds. She is the key to unleashing new sources of wealth and well-being."

Mulligan looked at Hoffman, who was looking at Mulligan.

"Isn't she, like, twelve years old, sir?" said Mulligan.

"How's she gonna do all that?" asked Hoffman.

Dr. Zimm's grin grew wider, like the one carved into a jack-o'-lantern that's started to rot a few days after Halloween.

"Her age imposes no limit on her mental capacity or her monetary potential, gentlemen. There is a reason her last name is Einstein."

Hoffman arched an eyebrow. "You know her family?"

"What I know, Herr Hoffman, is none of your concern. This, however, is."

He tapped the Return key on his computer.

"I received a Google alert early this morning, for any internet activity related to 'child prodigy,' 'Einstein,' 'physics,' 'quantum theory'—I've cast quite a wide net with my parameters and keywords. . . ."

"And?" said Mulligan. "You found the girl?"

"Oh, yes."

He clicked his mouse a few times. The screen filled with a full-color photo of a "child prodigy" named Paula Ehrenfest who had been lecturing on "Einstein" in a "physics" class at Columbia University. She was standing back while two burly bodyguards wrestled an unruly student to the floor of a lecture hall.

"You hit the trifecta," said Mulligan. "Three key words or phrases in one news story."

"Sweet," added Hoffman.

"It was on the front page of the Columbia University student newspaper," Dr. Zimm said proudly. "That, my friends, is Max Einstein. Even the alias she is using is a giveaway. Paul Ehrenfest was one of Albert Einstein's closest associates."

"You want we should head back to New York, Dr. Z?" asked Mulligan.

"Yes, Pinky. And take some additional associates with you. We don't want her slipping through our fingers again, do we?"

"No, sir."

"According to this article, Dr. Paula Ehrenfest is a

resident of John Jay Hall on the Columbia campus. I've already sent a map and directions to your phones. We must retrieve Max Einstein, re-educate her, and have her recommit to her true calling. We must help her realize who and where she is meant to be! She and I will do great work together. Great work indeed!"

11

The next morning in New York City, an unexpected visitor with an Irish accent showed up in the lobby of John Jay Hall.

"I'm lookin' for Max Einstein," the visitor told the Columbia University security guard stationed at a desk in the lobby.

"Sorry. There's no one here by that name."

"Oh, right. My bad. I believe she's registered as Adjunct Professor Paula Ehrenfest."

The guards had all been advised by Professor Ehrenfest's personal security detail to let them know if anyone suspicious ever showed up looking for her.

Especially if they uttered the words "Max Einstein."

"Let me check my computer," said the security guard.

The computer screen was facing her. The Irish-sounding visitor couldn't see it so only the guard knew that she had opened her Messages app and was quickly typing 10-25 and texting it to the two men stationed in the RV outside at the corner of 114th Street and Amsterdam Avenue.

"10-25" was police code for "Report in person."

"Is there some problem?" asked the Irish visitor.

"No," said the security guard. "Just having a little trouble locating Professor Ehrenfest's room number...."

Jamal and Danny came charging into the lobby. Fast.

"What's our situation, Edith?" asked Jamal.

Edith, the campus security guard, nodded at her freckle-faced, red-haired visitor.

"She was asking for Max Einstein."

"Because Max is my bloody friend," said Siobhan. "Who are you lot?"

"We work for Mr. Abercrombie," said Jamal.

"You mean, Ben? Well, I reckon I do, too. I'm Siobhan. Max and I are mates."

Danny held up his phone and snapped a photo of Siobhan's face. "Verifying identity with facial recognition software."

"Look, you two oafs, I need to talk to Max. I need her help."

"She's a match," said Danny after his phone played a

quick little confirmation melody. "Siobhan." (He pronounced her name correctly: sha-von.) "Member of the Change Makers team. Home country Ireland. Expert in geoscience. She views the earth as a patient whose maladies can be diagnosed through scientific examination, and eventually cured. She hopes, one day, to develop technology that will be able to predict major events such as earthquakes, hurricanes, and floods."

"Crikey," said Siobhan. "You found all that info about me online?"

"We're tied into the CMI database," explained Jamal.

"Oh. Does it also tell you that I like long walks on the beach at sunset?"

"Uh, no."

"Good, you dense fool eejit. Because I don't. Now where's Max?"

Jamal and Danny escorted Siobhan up to the seventh floor.

Max was so thrilled to see Siobhan, she threw her arms around her Irish friend and gave her a huge hug.

"Careful now, Max," grunted Siobhan. "I didn't fly all the way to New York City to have my ribs cracked."

Siobhan was fiery and fearless and had helped Max stand up to some extremely bad actors on the team's first mission in Africa.

"You two okay up here?" asked Jamal.

"We're better than okay," said Max, overjoyed to be reunited with her friend.

"You two can stand down," Siobhan told the bodyguards. "If anybody from the Corp shows up, they'll have to deal with me."

"We'll be on the street if you need us," said Danny.

"We'll let Mr. Abercrombie know you're here, Siobhan," added Jamal.

The guards headed out of the building.

Max closed her dorm room door.

"Okay, Siobhan, what's going on?" she asked.

"I need help. The earth back home is sick, Max. Very, very sick."

12

"All sorts of folks are getting seriously ill," said Siobhan. "I think there's something wrong with the earth underneath our village. Maybe all the way down to the water table."

"How many people have been affected?"

"When I left home, two dozen. Including my little brother, Séamus. He was weak as a kitten."

"I'm so sorry, Siobhan."

"Thank you for that, Max. But, if you don't mind, I'd like a little more than your sympathy. I'd like your brain."

"Well, to assess the situation and work up a solution, I think I'd need to be on the ground in Ireland."

"Exactly. There's a seven o'clock flight back to Dublin tonight—"

"I can't go."

"Excuse me?"

"Ben keeps telling me I need to lie low for a while."

"And since when did you start obeying the rules and what other people tell you?"

Max sighed. "The Corp and that crazy Dr. Zimm are still after me."

"Look, Max," said Siobhan, "I didn't fly all this way, on a ticket I paid for by myself, I'll have you know, just so I could hear you tell me 'no' to my face."

"But—"

"This is a real problem, Max. Not one of Dr. Einstein's famous thought experiments. I figured Ben would say no to you coming to Ireland, because of all this guff with the Corp. So I didn't even ask. I skipped the middle man and came straight to you. My home, my family—we need you, Max Einstein."

Max understood how Siobhan felt. With the theory of relativity, a lot of things depend on your perspective. For Siobhan, the problem back home in Ireland was currently the biggest problem in the whole world.

"You thirsty?" Max asked, abruptly shifting gears, hoping to buy a little time. She needed to figure out how to get Ben on board. This could be the CMI's new project. One of their own needed help!

"Excuse me?" said Siobhan. "What'd you say?"

"I asked if you're thirsty. I realized I've been a very rude host. I didn't offer you any kind of refreshment."

Siobhan's face softened a little. "I'll take a cold Coke if you have one. It's a scorcher out today."

"I know!" Max rummaged under her bed and found the sack of groceries she'd meant to unpack until something much more interesting—"Does reality really exist?"—had crossed her mind.

"I have Coke," she said. "But it's warm. Room temperature."

"Twenty-four degrees Celsius," said Siobhan.

"Seventy-five Fahrenheit," said Max.

"Well, it would take about twenty minutes to chill it to the proper drinking temperature in a freezer," said Siobhan. "If you put the can in a bucket of ice and add water to speed up the ice's melting and, therefore, its cooling ability, it'd be cold enough to drink in about six minutes."

Max nodded. "And if we add rock salt to the ice, the chill time would be reduced to just over two minutes."

"So, where's your bucket, ice, and salt?" said Siobhan.

"Sorry. It's a dorm, not a hotel." Max snapped her fingers. "Aha! Of course. Come on."

She tossed two warm cans of Coke to Siobhan.

"Where're we going?"

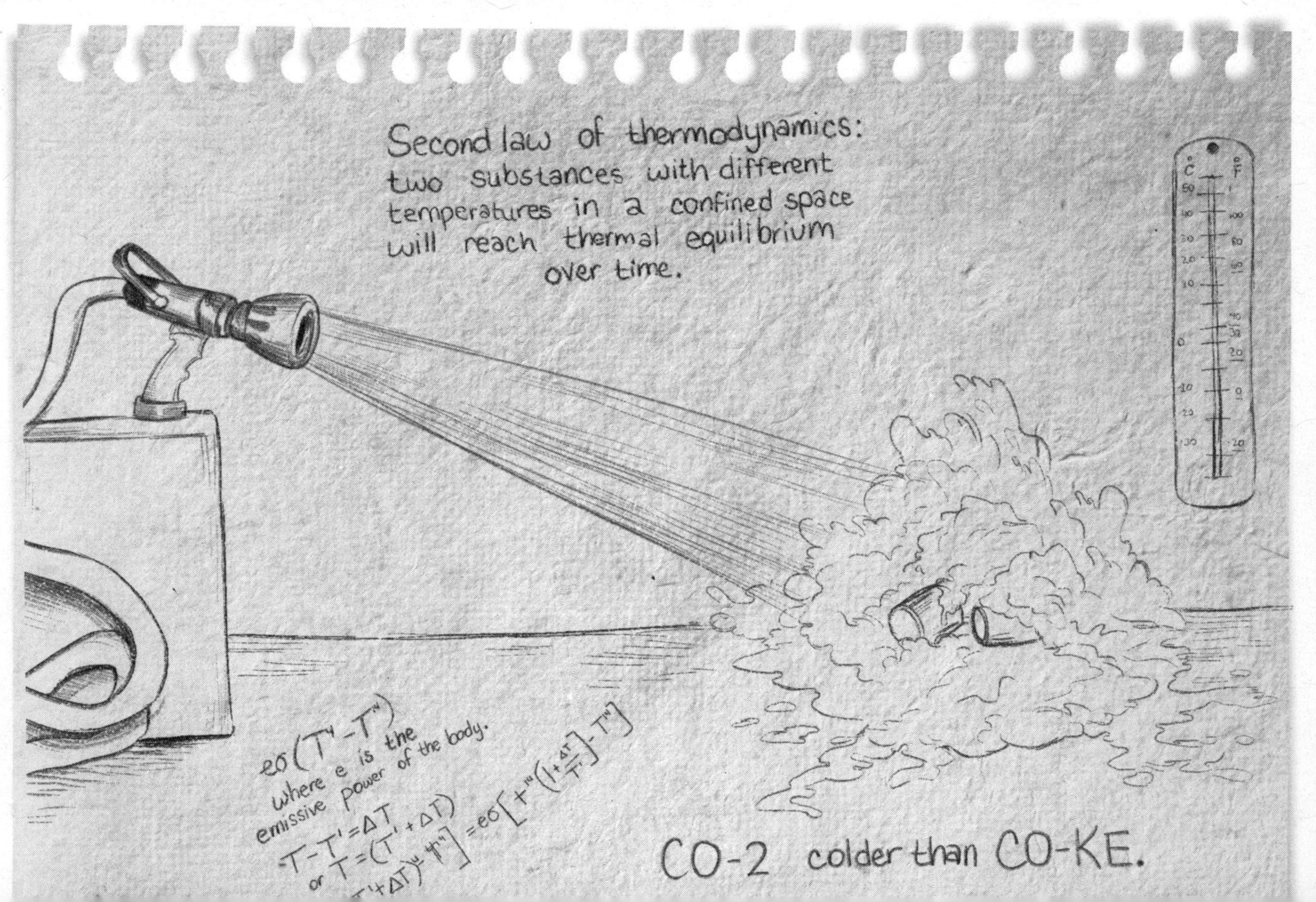

Second law of thermodynamics: two substances with different temperatures in a confined space will reach thermal equilibrium over time.
where e is the emissive power of the body.
CO-2 colder than CO-KE.

"Down the hall. There's a CO_2 fire extinguisher mounted on the wall. . . ."

Siobhan grinned. "Aha, indeed! An excellent idea!"

They hurried out the door. As it closed, Max bent down to place a small metal washer on the floor directly in front of the door's sill.

"Max?" said Siobhan. "What are you doing?"

"Sorry. Little home security hack."

"Can we hack the Coke cans first? Talking about how thirsty I am made me even thirstier!"

Max led Siobhan to the fire extinguisher cabinet.

They placed the two Coke cans on the floor, aimed the extinguisher's nozzle, and pulled the trigger.

When the frosty fog cleared, Siobhan and Max cleaned and popped open their cans.

"Ah! Five degrees Celsius!" said Siobhan. "Perfect."

Max took a sip and agreed. "Good thing thermodynamics has laws!"

"This university has laws, too!" shouted a voice behind them.

Nancy Hanker.

13

"One kid on my floor was bad enough," screamed the resident adviser. "Two? That's it. You're out of here, Little Miss Sunshine."

Siobhan, who'd been chugging her cold Coke, burped a long, gassy rumbler in Nancy Hanker's face.

"Sorry," said Siobhan with a smirk. "Natural release of pressure. Did you know that cows also burp?"

"No," said Nancy, waving at the air in front of her nose.

"Huh," said Siobhan. "Figured you might be familiar with cows and all their bodily functions...."

"Come on," said Max.

"Where we goin'?" asked Siobhan.

"Downstairs. We'll come back with Jamal and Danny."

"I'm not afraid of your two overgrown goons!" said Nancy. "Neither is Columbia University!"

"They might ought to be," said Siobhan. "I know those two blokes scared me a wee bit when I first met 'em."

"Come on, Siobhan," said Max. "We'll take the steps. And Nancy?"

"Yes?"

"Please don't touch anything in my room."

"It's not *your* room anymore," said Nancy.

"Let's wait to hear what the chair of the physics department says after he receives a call from a very generous donor named Benjamin Abercrombie."

"Too right," said Siobhan. Then she burped again.

The two friends clanked their way down the fire steps. They pushed open the exit door and stepped out into the muggy air.

"There's their command center," said Max, pointing to the RV parked at the curb on 114th Street.

"Hope it's air-conditioned," said Siobhan.

"Once we settle this," said Max, leading the way up the sidewalk, "we'll figure out what to do about your situation back home in—"

Max did not complete that thought.

Because two men came out of the RV.

And neither one was Jamal or Danny.

"This way," said Max, ducking her head. She turned on her heel and picked up her pace.

"Who are those nasty-looking blokes?" whispered Siobhan.

"The same two who ransacked my old apartment."

"What?"

"They work for the Corp. Mr. Weinstock—he's a friend of Charl and Isabl—showed me security camera footage of those two tearing my old place apart."

"You really *are* being hunted."

"Yeah."

"I thought maybe you were just making that guff up because you didn't want to fly all the way to Dublin."

"Actually, I wish I had completely mastered the mechanics of quantum entanglement so we could teleport our body particles over to Ireland right now!"

Max chanced a glance over her shoulder. A black SUV that had been parked behind Jamal and Danny's rolling command center pulled away from the curb. Fast.

As it passed, a piercing beam of sunlight sliced through the tinted windows. Max could make out two familiar silhouettes in the backseat.

Jamal and Danny. It looked like their hands were cuffed behind their backs.

"There's more of them," said Max. "And they have Jamal and Danny."

"Where to?" asked Siobhan.

Max couldn't decide.

"Hey!" shouted a man with an Irish accent. "It's her. The girl with all the curly hair."

Yeah, that was the bad thing about Max's wildly tangled moptop. It made her extremely easy to spot in a crowd—even at a distance of fifty yards, which is all she and Siobhan had on the two Corp enforcers.

"Don't let her get away!" shouted the other man.

"Siobhan?" said Max. "They only want me. You should run for it."

"Right. Like that's going to happen. Where to, fearless leader?"

Max scanned the buildings.

"We'll cut through the library and hit the quad."

"Reckon we won't have time to pick up a good book...."

"Maybe next time."

The two friends took off.

The two men came running after them.

Max and Siobhan raced into the library, ran through

the stacks and the study carrels, and exited on the far side of the building, which put them on the grassy quad in the center of the Columbia campus.

"They're gaining on us," said Siobhan. "Speed equals distance over time. Over time, they will decrease their distance from us because they are speedier."

"Physics!" said Max. "Good idea!"

"What?"

"Come on. We need a little instantaneous velocity! There's a lab I know. Did some wave work inside it."

Max and Siobhan kicked their bodies into hyperdrive and, charging through a maze of building entrances and exits, finally made it into the physics building. The two goons were still behind them, but a little farther back.

"Here we go," said Max, opening a door to a lab. "They have a signal-generating transmitter we can borrow."

"For what?"

"To make a sonic weapon!"

"As in sonic boom?"

"Nope. They won't hear a thing. But they'll definitely feel it!"

14

Max quickly wired the transmitter to a subwoofer.

"Help me drag that wooden crate over here," she said to Siobhan. "We'll put the speaker inside for a bigger blast. Turn it into a sonic cannon."

Siobhan and Max shoved the empty box across the floor, propped open its lid, and hefted the heavy subwoofer into it. Max connected a string of wires from the transmitter to an amplifier and then to the speaker.

"Max?" whispered Siobhan. She was kneeling at the door, peering out into the hall.

"Yeah?"

"Those two rumbly blokes are trying every doorknob in the building. They'll be on us in a flash."

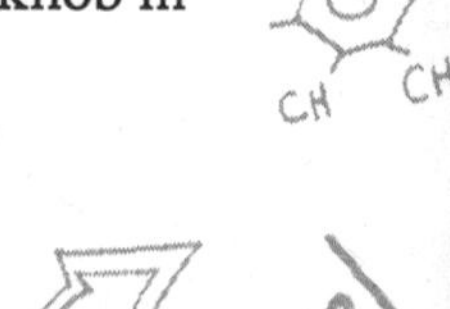

"Here," said Max. "Found these over near the goggles. Put 'em on."

"Headphones?"

"*Noise-canceling* headphones."

"To protect us from what?"

"The non-lethal weapon we just created."

Siobhan looked confused. "When, exactly, did we do that?"

"Just now. This transmitter will generate waves between 5 and 9 hertz—"

"Below the low end of the typical human audible range, 20 hertz," said Siobhan.

"Correct. We'll pump those waves out at a high level, even though the sound will be inaudible. Frequencies below the limit of human hearing are felt by the human body, not heard. The infrasonic attack will cause a liquid-filled compartment in any uncovered ears to suddenly swell. That'll cause vertigo, tinnitus, and other nasty stuff. We'll immobilize our two targets without causing any permanent or severe damage."

"Well, aren't we nice?"

"Not if we hit the brown note."

"What's that?"

"A hypothetical infrasonic frequency that would cause humans to lose control of their bowels due to resonance."

"They'll poop their pants?"

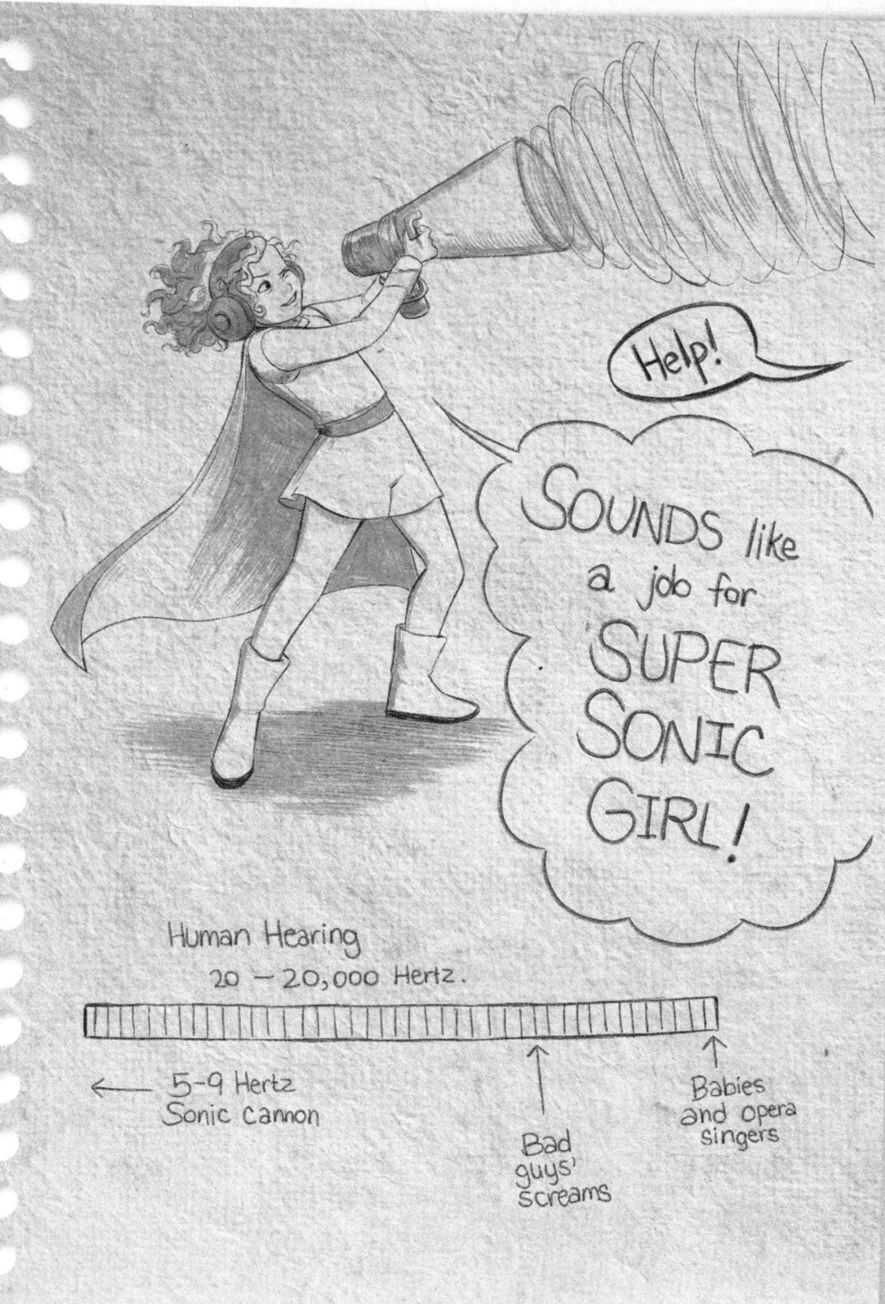
Help!
SOUNDS like a job for SUPER SONIC GIRL!
Human Hearing
20 – 20,000 Hertz.
← 5-9 Hertz
Sonic cannon
Bad guys' screams
Babies and opera singers

"Theoretically," said Max.

"Give me that headgear!" said Siobhan. "I only packed one extra pair of knickers in my kit...."

Max and Siobhan slipped on their headsets just as the lab door burst open.

"There you are!" snarled the man with the Irish accent.

Max flipped a switch. She and Siobhan fled the room.

There was no sound but plenty of subsonic waves.

The two men's hands flew up to their heads. Their eyeballs went shaky. Their legs, rubbery.

The one with the Irish accent grabbed the seat of his pants and had a very embarrassed expression on his face.

Both men wilted and crumbled to the floor.

"They probably won't know who or where they are until we're long gone," said Max as she and Siobhan tossed their headgear into a recycling bin in the lobby of the physics building.

"So where do we go now?" said Siobhan.

"First, back to my room. I need to grab a few things."

"What? Max, are you mad? Those two know where you live. That means the Corp knows where you live. Plus, they hijacked your bodyguards...."

"True. But I think we have thirty minutes to an hour before those quivering lumps feel like chasing us again."

“One of them had an Irish accent,” said Siobhan as they made their way back across the campus quad.

“Yeah,” said Max. “I noticed that. Made me wonder if the Corp is after you instead of me.”

“Nah. I’m not the Chosen One,” joked Siobhan.

“Right.”

“Okay. We go back to your room. You grab your things. Then where do we go?”

“How about Ireland? I hear there’s a village that could use some girl power.”

“Works for me.”

“I’d need to tell Ben about Jamal and Danny being abducted.”

“Your guards looked like ex–military commandos,” said Siobhan. “I reckon they can handle themselves. Wouldn’t be surprised if they already escaped.”

“Let’s hope so.”

Retracing their steps, they reached John Jay Hall.

“Come on,” said Max. “We’ll take the stairs.”

“Up seven flights?”

“We’ll avoid the lobby . . . and any Corp goons who might be lurking in it.”

“Good point.”

Max led the way up.

"Wish I had another Coke," said Siobhan, panting heavily as they rounded the sixth-floor landing.

"One more flight," said Max.

"Lead on, boss."

They made it to the seventh floor.

"I need my suitcase," said Max, heading up the hall.

"The one with all the Einstein memorabilia and books?" said Siobhan, who remembered Max's portable bookcase from the CMI team's first mission.

"Yeah. That one photo of Einstein is the first thing I remember from back when I was—"

Max raised her right hand to signal "halt." She pressed her finger to her lips.

The metal washer Max had placed on the floor earlier was now dangling off the magnet she'd affixed to the bottom of her door.

It was a simple "burglar alarm." If someone swung open the door while she was out, the magnet would pass over and pick up the metal washer.

Max turned to Siobhan and silently mouthed, *Someone is in my room!*

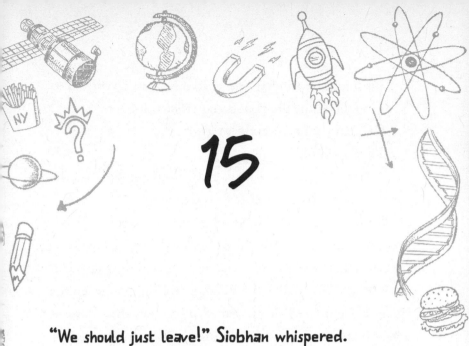

15

"We should just leave!" Siobhan whispered.

Max shook her head. "Not without my suitcase."

But who was inside her dorm room? Her security detail? More Corp heavies in black suits? The annoying resident adviser, stripping Max's bed and tossing her belongings into a trash heap, making the room nice and tidy for its new resident?

But the suitcase was her most prized possession. In fact, it was just about her only possession, except for her clothes and floppy trench coat (she'd be sure to grab that, too). The suitcase was her only link to her past. It was her whole history.

Max sometimes did things on impulse that she regretted later.

This might be another one of those times.

She grabbed the doorknob and twisted it open.

"Hi, guys," said a friendly voice.

"Tisa?" said Max.

"What are you doing here, girl?" asked Siobhan as the three friends flew together for a group hug.

Tisa was another member of Max's CMI team. A biochemist from Kenya (she already had a PhD at age thirteen), her father was one of the wealthiest industrialists in all of Africa. Tisa had stood by Max and Siobhan when the three of them faced down armed pirates on their African adventure. That sort of terrifying, high-adrenaline situation can make people friends for life. It definitely did with Max, Siobhan, and Tisa.

"How did you get into my room?" asked Max.

"That credit card trick with the lock you taught me. Remember?"

"Oh," said Max. "Right. Your dad's rich. You have credit cards...."

Tisa laughed.

"But how'd you know what room Max was in?" asked Siobhan.

"CMI gave me her mailing address," said Tisa.

"Snail mail?" said Siobhan. "That's so twentieth century."

"I know," said Tisa with a bright smile. "But I wanted to send Max a small gift from our friends in Lubumbashi. They really love their solar-powered electricity."

"They sent me a hand-sewn Einstein doll," said Max. "It's in my suitcase."

"Which," said Siobhan, "you need to grab immediately."

"And my coat."

"Good idea. It was raining when I left Ireland." Siobhan turned to Tisa. "We can't be here. There are several goons from the Corp gunning for Max. We believe one is currently changing into clean underpants."

"Excuse me?" said Tisa.

"Long story," said Max, closing her antique Einstein suitcase and snapping the clasps shut. "Grab your backpack, Siobhan."

"Right-o."

"All I have are these," said Tisa, indicating a matching pair of rolling bags.

"Planning on an extended stay in the States?" said Siobhan.

"No, Siobhan. I want to go with you and Max to Ireland."

"You were serious?" said Siobhan, softening.

"Yeah."

Siobhan turned to Max. "We've been texting."

"I'm the one who encouraged Siobhan to come here to convince you to join us, even if Ben doesn't give us an official stamp of approval," added Tisa. "This is exactly the sort of thing the CMI is meant to do! The world's not going to save itself, Max."

"Ben!" said Max.

"Huh?" said Tisa and Siobhan.

Max pulled out her special phone. "This is an emergency. He might know a safe spot for us to spend the night."

"That seven o'clock flight to Dublin," said Siobhan.

"I'll suggest it," said Max with a grin as she dialed the benefactor's private number.

Ben didn't like the idea of "flying commercial" to Ireland. He, as usual, had other ideas.

"Go see Mr. Weinstock. Your usual rendezvous point."

"Okay. But, Ben?"

"Yes, Max?"

"We really should help Siobhan's village in Ireland."

"I will take your suggestion under advisement and give it serious consideration, Max."

Yeah. Sometimes Ben sounded more like he was forty instead of fourteen.

"I'm worried about Jamal and Danny," Max told him.

"They're fine. They're currently at the New York Police

Department's 26th Precinct helping file charges against their two would-be kidnappers."

"They escaped?"

"Yes," said Ben. "It took all of fifteen minutes. I only hire the best, Max. Go to the rendezvous. The Corp knows about your dorm room. You're not safe anywhere on the Columbia campus."

"Where *will* we be safe?"

"Mr. Weinstock has your answer. Good luck."

"You want to say anything to Siobhan and Tisa?" Max asked. "They're both here, too."

"No, thank you," said Ben, who wasn't too big on social interaction. "Enjoy the rest of your day."

Yeah. Exactly the wrong thing to say. Ben did that a lot.

Max, Siobhan, and Tisa toted their luggage down the stairwell and headed east to the 116th Street subway station.

"We'll take the C train to West 4th," Max told her friends. "It's right near Washington Square Park."

As the three friends fled Columbia with their few possessions, Max, once again, felt a connection to Albert Einstein. Sure, he was a genius, a theoretical physicist, and a Nobel laureate. But he was also a refugee. A Jew who had to flee Germany when the Nazis declared his discoveries to be "un-German." He came to the United States where he sometimes had mixed feelings about his comfortable and privileged life in Princeton, New Jersey. "I am almost ashamed to be living in such a place while all the rest struggle and suffer," he wrote.

Max sort of felt the same way about her time hiding out at Columbia.

Except, in the end, she really didn't have a place to live.

Just a place to flee.

16

"She escaped?" Dr. Zimm shouted at his secure speakerphone. *"Again?"*

"She did something weird to us," said Mr. Mulligan.

"Made one of us go boom-boom in our underpants," added Mr. Hoffman.

"You were moaning and groaning on the floor, too!" shouted Mr. Mulligan.

"Maybe. But I didn't mess myself. . . ."

"Enough," seethed Dr. Zimm. "What about the rest of your team?"

"They've, uh, been detained by the local police," admitted Mr. Mulligan. "That Max Einstein has some very talented private bodyguards."

Yes, thought Dr. Zimm. *Maybe we should recruit them for the Corp.*

"You want us to go back to her dorm?" asked Mr. Mulligan. "Grab her there?"

"She isn't there," the young guest in Dr. Zimm's office said with a giggle. "She's smart. It would be dumb for her to return to a location known to her pursuers. Max Einstein is a genius. Therefore, she is not at Columbia."

There was silence on the other side of the phone.

"Who's that, Dr. Z?" Mr. Mulligan finally asked.

"Lenard," said Dr. Zimm. "He is my new... assistant."

Lenard giggled again.

"Stand by for further instructions, gentlemen," said Dr. Zimm.

He switched off the speakerphone and swiveled in his chair to face the humanoid named Lenard. He was a robot, yes, but eerily realistic. He resembled a thirteen-year-old boy with waxy black hair that seemed to have melted over the top of his mannequin head. Lenard had been built with extremely flexible skin, expressive eyes, and highly realistic facial features.

The better for him to work with Max Einstein, once she was in the Corp's clutches.

That was the master plan. To team Max Einstein up with the most sophisticated, artificial intelligence–powered robot on the planet. The Corp was keenly interested in quantum computing. With Max and Lenard working together, they had a chance to completely control the revolutionary new technology (not to mention all the money it would generate)!

Dr. Zimm had convinced the bot engineers to make Lenard "physically and aesthetically pleasing" to a twelve-year-old girl. That's why they'd modeled his face after that of the latest teen idol singing sensation. His body—an articulated metal frame coursing with wires—was covered in trendy sweat clothes. As for his annoying and inappropriate giggles? That, according to the Corp bot engineers, was "a minor glitch."

"Where is she, Lenard?" Dr. Zimm asked his humanoid companion. "Where is Max Einstein?"

"You are familiar with my operating system?" asked Lenard.

"Yes," said Dr. Zimm. "You work by machine learning coupled with text and data mining. We feed you data. You examine that content and find patterns."

"Correct. I am only as intelligent as my data diet. I only know what I am fed. Garbage in, garbage out."

"But we didn't feed you garbage, Lenard."

"Correct. In fact, I have been given access to every security camera in New York City. With my facial recognition software, I can easily identify and isolate Max Einstein and her movements. Are you interested in where she was last Tuesday?"

"Not really..."

"Buying six cans of Coca-Cola and some Pringles at the Appletree Market at 1226 Amsterdam Avenue," said Lenard. Then he giggled, as if he found the street address to be, somehow, funny. "Pringles. An American brand of stackable snack chips made from dehydrated potato particles."

"I am not interested in where Max was last Tuesday or, for that matter, Pringles," said Dr. Zimm, trying his best to sound like the patient father of a brainy son. "Where is she *now*?"

"Cross-referencing all internal data, I can project her probable current location with a confidence level of ninety-eight point nine percent." Another giggle.

"Where?"

"Washington Square Park. She often goes there after high-stress encounters to play chess with an old man in a floppy cap. I am reviewing surveillance videos. Buffering. Buffering. She calls the old man Mr. Weinstock, if I am reading her lips correctly, which, of course, I am. My lip-reading software is quite advanced. Would you like to play chess, Dr. Zimm?"

"No, thank you, Lenard. I need to make another phone call."

"Of course. You will be contacting Mr. Mulligan and Mr. Hoffman and advising them to immediately apprehend Max Einstein in Washington Square Park."

"Yes. You are correct."

"I usually am. Especially when analyzing the patterns of extremely predictable human beings such as you, Dr. Zimm."

And then Lenard giggled—for a full five minutes.

17

Max, Siobhan, and Tisa raced out of the subway and headed over to Washington Square Park.

Mr. Weinstock wasn't there!

"That's where we usually meet," said Max, gesturing toward an empty chess table mounted on an iron pedestal. No one was sitting on the benches on either side. Other tables were occupied. Games were being played. But Mr. Weinstock wasn't one of the players.

In the distance, Max saw the silhouette of two shady figures marching along the park's paths. Their eyes were glued to the phones they held in their hands. Siobhan saw them, too.

"It's those same two blokes again," she said. "The ones who chased Max and me across the campus."

"How'd they know where to find you guys?" asked Tisa.

"Judging by the way they're studying their phones," whispered Max, "there must be an app for that."

"Do you think your Mr. Weinstock set us up?" asked Siobhan, balling her fists in anger. "Is he playing for the Corp team, too?"

"Doubtful," said Max.

"What should we do?" asked Tisa.

Max looked to the street. Saw a motorcycle leaning against the curb.

Too bad she didn't know how to start a motorcycle without a key. Plus, three people probably couldn't fit on the one seat.

Suddenly, a convertible screeched to a stop.

"Max?" shouted Isabl. She, of course, was behind the wheel. She was an incredibly skilled driver. If Isabl didn't work for the CMI, she could've done car stunts in Hollywood. Charl was riding shotgun. Literally. Chances were, he had some sort of concealed weapon up front in the passenger seat with him.

Max was glad to see Charl and Isabl. On the other hand, she wasn't so glad that Isabl had shouted her name because the two hit men from the Corp had heard it, too. They lowered their phones and came charging across the park.

"Head for the convertible," Max shouted at Siobhan and Tisa. "Go!"

They took off running.

Max quickly surveyed her surroundings.

She recognized some of the other chess players. Including Squeegie, a guy with a nasty temper and a very short fuse.

"Sorry about this, you guys," she muttered as she ran along the tables swinging her suitcase and the flaps of her overcoat to knock off all the playing pieces she could. Pawns, kings, queens, rooks, bishops—they all went flying to the pavement.

"Why, you little . . . !" shouted Squeegie.

He and about a dozen other very serious, very angry chess players leaped up from their tables and started tearing after Max. She ran straight at the two bad guys coming at her from the opposite direction.

The mob of angry chess players was running behind her. The two goons were running toward her. It was time to apply Newton's third law of motion.

When the two groups pursuing her were maybe three feet apart, Max ducked and darted sharply to the left.

The chess players and team of Corp heavies did not.

There was a collision, resulting in equal and opposite force being applied to the two colliding objects. In other words, people ended up on their butts.

Max dashed up the sidewalk, tossed her suitcase into

the backseat of the convertible, and climbed in with her friends.

"We need to not be here!" she shouted.

"Roger that," said Isabl, slamming the gas pedal down to the floorboard.

"Sorry we were late," shouted Charl over the screaming engine as the convertible rocketed away from the park. "We thought you guys might be hungry. We stopped to grab food. It's in the sack back there...."

"Where's Mr. Weinstock?" asked Max.

"Safe," said Charl. "Ben took care of that, too."

Isabl slid the car into a screeching turn down Broadway.

"Uh-oh," said Tisa. She had craned around and was looking behind the fast-moving convertible.

At a faster-moving motorcycle.

One of the Corp guys, the one with the snarling tattoo on his neck, was only half a block behind them.

Unlike Max, the man knew how to start a motorcycle without a key.

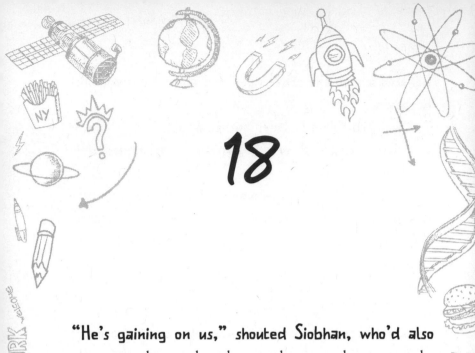

18

"He's gaining on us," shouted Siobhan, who'd also spun around to gawk at the crazed man on the motorcycle.

Isabl bobbed and weaved the sporty convertible through the thick traffic clogging New York City's main artery. The motorcycle was able to zig and zag and match her every move.

"Isabl?" cried Max. "Do you have a mobile infrared transmitter?"

"You mean a traffic signal pre-emptor?" said Charl. "Those are illegal."

"Not for emergency vehicles," said Max. "And, if you ask me, this is an emergency."

"And this is a vehicle," said Isabl. She reached down and grabbed a small black box mounted on suction cups. She

slapped it against the windshield and flicked a switch. The box started whirring and clicking.

"What the blazes is that?" shouted Siobhan as the convertible roared and screamed down Broadway, approaching a red light.

"A twelve-volt-powered strobe light that can change traffic signals from red to green at a distance of fifteen hundred feet," explained Max.

"Get out," said Tisa. "That's impossible."

The light turned green.

"Mobile infrared transmitters were invented more than twenty years ago," explained Max as best she could over the rush of wind that sent her mop of curls bouncing like a wild clump of inflatable air dancers outside a used car lot. "MITs were created so emergency personnel in ambulances, police cars, and fire trucks could get where they needed to be faster."

Another light switched from red to green.

"Isn't science fun?" said Siobhan with a laugh.

One by one, the traffic lights down Broadway obeyed the strobing commands of Isabl's device.

"All right," said Max. "We have our uninterrupted forward momentum. Now we just have to use it to take care of this guy behind us."

"I have an idea," said Charl, reaching into his black commando jacket.

"We can't shoot him, you fool eejit!" said Siobhan. "We're surrounded by innocent civilians."

"We don't need a gun or bullets," said Max. "We have these!"

She reached into the large paper sack from Burger King.

"Cheeseburgers?" said Tisa.

"Double Whoppers with cheese," said Charl.

"Perfect," said Max. "Force equals mass times acceleration."

"You want me to accelerate?"

"Nope. Just keep it steady."

Isabl kept the swerving to a minimum as the traffic lights strung across the Broadway intersections continued to change from red to green.

"Unwrap your ammunition," said Max, handing a Whopper to Tisa and Siobhan. "Remove the top bun. Line up your shot."

The motorcycle guy rocked his wrist and gave his whining engine all the gas it could guzzle.

"Here he comes!" shouted Tisa. "He's gaining on us."

"Wait for it," Max urged calmly. "Wait for it."

The motorcycle was only ten feet behind the convertible. The rider reached down into his belt.

The Cheeseburger Defense

Beef patties = meaty blindfolds.

Cheese for extra adhesion.

Special sauce. Very sticky.

F = MA.

Force = Mass x Acceleration

F also equals KB — KaBoom!

"He has a weapon!" shrieked Tisa.

"So do we!" shouted Max. "Fire at will!"

The three sloppy cheeseburgers went flying backward.

Two of the flying cheeseburgers were direct hits. They smacked the motorcycle man, who wasn't wearing a helmet, right in his face. Their sticky all-beef patties became meaty blindfolds cheese-glued to his eyes. Not able to see where he was going, the motorcycle rider swerved into a skid and, sliding sideways, slammed into a fire hydrant, where he wiped out with a bounce and a rolling tumble.

"His bike's down but he's up on his feet," said Tisa, as the convertible continued to streak down Broadway. "He's okay."

"So are we!" said Siobhan.

"For now," said Max. "They'll come after us again. No place in New York is safe."

Charl turned around to face the three geniuses in the backseat. "And that's why, the next time the Corp tries to grab you, you guys won't be here."

19

Isabl removed the traffic-signal switcher from the windshield as soon as the motorcycle was off the convertible's tail.

"No need to drive like a maniac anymore," said Charl.

"Yeah," said Isabl, easing off the gas. "Too bad."

"So," said Max, as the convertible cruised along the shoreline of Brooklyn. "If New York City isn't safe for us anymore, where do we go?"

"Ben has an idea," said Charl.

"What is it?" asked Max.

"He'd rather tell you himself."

"Fine. Let's give him a call."

"No need," said Isabl. "He's waiting for us."

"Where?"

"Long Island. We should be there in thirty minutes. Faster if I use my little blinking box again..."

"Isabl..." said Charl.

"Fine. Like I said: We should be there in thirty minutes."

Half an hour later, the convertible passed a security checkpoint and pulled through the chain-link gate of a private airstrip. A sleek jet was sitting on the runway. A stretch limousine was parked beside it. There were two tents set up in the parking lot—the kind you'd see at a fancy outdoor party.

"That's Mr. Abercrombie's newest, fastest jet," said Charl.

"What's with the tents?" asked Siobhan.

"Guess Ben wants to feed you guys, too," said Isabl, nodding toward a server in a tuxedo carrying a silver tray filled with steaming food. The nearest tent, its side flaps open, was set up like an outdoor dining room.

"Good," said Tisa. "I'm starving. And we're all out of cheeseburgers."

The door on the jet folded open and became a staircase. A few seconds later, Ben, the awkward fourteen-year-old billionaire who'd set up the Change Makers Institute, shuffled down the steps, his eyes lowered, as if he were studying his shoelaces.

"That's the benefactor?" whispered Tisa.

"Yeah," said Max. "His real name is Ben."

"Your fella's a fine-lookin' thing," said Siobhan.

"He's not my fella," said Max, her cheeks flushing nearly as red as her hair.

Everybody piled out of the convertible. Tisa and Siobhan, who'd never met Ben, raced each other across the tarmac, each hoping to be the first to shake the benefactor's hand. Max grinned and followed after them. Charl and Isabl headed into the tent, where they'd spied a huge urn of coffee.

"Good evening, sir," Tisa said to Ben. (She'd won the footrace.) "It is truly an honor to meet you."

She held out her hand. Ben stuffed both of his hands into the pockets of his jeans.

"Thanks," he mumbled. "Great."

"I'm Tisa."

"Yeah. I recognized you. We have photos. In the database."

"And I'm Siobhan, sir. Or should I call you Ben?"

Ben shrugged. "I don't know. Up to you."

Finally looking up, the benefactor peered between the two girls right in front of him and saw Max standing behind them. He smiled.

"Hey, Max. Hungry?"

"Yeah."

"Cool. You're eating with me." He gestured toward the

smaller of the two catering tents. "Chef Henri has prepared dinner. For all of us. You like lobster rolls?"

"Never had one," said Max.

"I love them," said Ben. "Especially with a pickle and potato chips." He turned to Tisa and Siobhan. "You guys are with Charl and Isabl over there."

"Ooh," teased Siobhan. "You and Max are having yourselves a private little dinner date, eh?"

"No," said Ben. "We just need to talk. Discuss stuff."

"And eat lobster rolls," said Tisa.

"Right. They're on your menu, too. Max?"

Ben gestured toward the smaller tent, which looked like something you'd see set up for a sultan's desert caravan. Inside, there was a crystal chandelier dangling from the center of the silky ceiling. The small table was covered with linen, shimmering silverware, and amazingly expensive-looking china.

"Nice picnic," said Max. "Most people just go with paper plates and plastic forks."

"Most people aren't billionaires," said Ben.

"True."

"I hope I wasn't rude to Tisa and Siobhan."

Max squeezed her thumb close to her index finger to indicate about an inch. "Little bit."

"Sorry about that. I'm not really a people person."

"I know. But—you are a person who likes to *help* people. That might be more important."

"Thank you." He pulled off the shiny domed lid on a serving platter. "Lobster roll?"

"Thanks."

Max and Ben both bit into the chunky lobster salad riding inside a soft, split-top hot dog bun.

"Did you know," said Ben, "that lobster was so plentiful in colonial times that it was only served to household servants and prisoners?"

Max nodded. Of course she knew that. She and Ben were nerds. They knew all sorts of stuff nobody else really knew or cared about.

"In the late 1800s," said Max, "lobster was considered the poor person's chicken. Boston baked beans cost fifty-three cents a pound. Lobster? Eleven cents a pound."

They both nodded and munched some more.

"So, Max, you want to go to Ireland and help Siobhan?" said Ben.

"Yes. Tisa does, too."

"Good. I've arranged a flight for you three. Plus Charl and Isabl. You'll have my full financial support. Anything you need, just let me know."

"Thank you, Ben. This means a lot to us. To me."

Ben looked down at his plate and pushed his potato chips into a tidy pile.

"You're welcome," he said. "Besides, it's safer for you out of New York right now. And Max?"

"Yeah?"

"Thank you."

"For what?"

Ben looked up from his plate and held Max's gaze. "Everything."

20

When Max and Ben finished their meal, they rejoined the others in the larger tent.

"Um, Charl?" said Ben. "Isabl? Can you guys tell everybody the plan? Fill them in on the details and stuff? I, uh, need to leave."

"Are you taking that spiffy jet?" asked Siobhan.

"No. That's for you guys. I'll, uh, take the limo. I have a business meeting in New York tomorrow. I might talk to some people at the UN, too. We'll see. We're working on plans for some major projects. Okay. Gotta go. Have fun in Ireland. Don't kiss the Blarney Stone. It's really a big rock. Rocks are dirty. You shouldn't kiss dirt."

And, with that, Ben hurried off to the limousine where

his driver stood ready to whisk him off to wherever he wanted to be whisked.

"We're going to Ireland?" Tisa asked Max.

"Yep! You, me, Siobhan, Charl, and Isabl."

"Smashing," said Siobhan. "Traveling with company makes a journey fly."

"So does a jet," cracked Tisa.

"Right you are."

Charl stood up to address the group. "We think—and Ben agrees—that this Irish mission couldn't've come at a better time. It'll keep Max off the Corp's radar here in the states until we can plug the leak at CMI. Once we do that, we can move on to our next full-group project."

"There's a leak?" said Siobhan.

"We think so," said Isabl. "They know too much about Max's whereabouts—and not just today. Someone must be feeding them information."

"Probably that dodgy lady in Jerusalem," said Siobhan. "You know, the stern one who was always looking at us funny."

"It isn't Ms. Kaplan," said Charl. "Or anybody else at HQ."

"They've all been cleared," added Isabl. "Anyway, we're coming with you guys. To fly the plane."

"And to provide protection," added Charl. "We don't think the Corp knows about our decision to extract Max, but we do know, through our own spies and informants, that they have invested heavily in the most sophisticated, technologically advanced, human tracker ever created. They've given it the code name LENARD AI."

"They're using artificial intelligence to track Max?" said Tisa.

Isabl nodded. "We think that's how they knew you three would be in Washington Square Park. There wasn't enough time for Max's location to have been leaked. They must've fed their computer some excellent raw data. Probably accessed NYPD security cameras and ran their facial recognition software to isolate Max, track her movements, predict her routines."

"I did go visit Mr. Weinstock down in Washington Square Park at least once or twice a week," admitted Max.

"In high-stress situations?" asked Tisa.

"Usually," said Max. "Or when I just needed to blow off a little steam. I guess the Corp computer figured that out."

"Crikey," said Siobhan. "I can't believe they've been tracking you like that."

"Fortunately," said Charl, "none of their data mining would indicate that you frequently visit Ireland."

"If it does," said Max, "it's not any kind of intelligence, artificial or otherwise. It's just dumb. I've never been to Ireland."

"Exactly," said Isabl. "And that's why we think it'll be a safe haven."

"Unless you drink the water in my village," said Siobhan. "Then you won't be so safe. You'll be clutching your gut and running to the loo."

"The restroom?" said Max.

Siobhan nodded. "That's where I think the problem lies."

"In the bathroom?" said Tisa.

"No. The water. Most of the illnesses have been gastrointestinal. You know—vomiting, diarrhea, cholera, dysentery..."

Tisa pushed away her half-nibbled lobster roll.

"I'm not so hungry anymore," she mumbled.

"Neither is anyone back home," said Siobhan.

"You guys?" said Max, hoping to inject some optimism into the conversation. "You want to hear something that's kind of amazing?"

"Sure," said Tisa. "As long as it's not about diarrhea."

"No. I promise. But get this: The same water has been on Earth for millions and millions of years. It just keeps getting evaporated up into the clouds until they're so heavy they dump rain, which fills the lakes and rivers, which evaporates again, and heads back up into the clouds. No matter how dirty we make it, water can always become clean again, eventually. Nature takes care of itself over a very, very long time. The trick is to speed up the process."

"Stow your gear on board, guys," said Charl, glancing at his high-tech watch. "We want to be wheels-up in ten minutes!"

Siobhan raised her bottle of crystal-clear water. "I can't thank you lot enough for lending a hand," she said. *"Sláinte mhaith!"*

"Huh?" said Tisa. " 'Sloncha' what now?"

"It's an old Irish toast in Gaelic. *Sláinte mhaith!* It means, 'good health.' "

Max raised her water glass. "*Sláinte mhaith!* Which, hopefully, is exactly what we're going to bring to your hometown, Siobhan."

21

Dr. Zimm took a deep breath before stepping through the tall doorway leading into the Corp's boardroom.

Lenard did not. The robot simply whirred into the shadowy room behind Dr. Zimm, trailing him like an eager teenager on "Take Your Humanoid to Work Day."

Twelve severe-looking men and women ringed the boardroom's massive mahogany table. Their stern faces belonged to representatives of Big Banking, Big Tech, Big Pharma, Big Defense, Big Media. If an industry was Big, with global reach and limitless greed, it fought for a seat at this particular table. The world's wealthiest companies joined forces to form the Corp for one reason and one reason only: to grow even wealthier. The billionaires on the

board did not like being disappointed by the people they hired to help them make their fortunes grow.

People like Dr. Zacchaeus Zimm.

"The girl continues to elude you?" said the pink-faced chairman. He was furious. So were all the others.

"For the moment, yes," said Dr. Zimm as calmly as he could. He'd been steeling himself for this face-to-face inquisition ever since he received the call to "report immediately" to the Corp's top-secret headquarters located in the mountains of West Virginia. The boardroom was, actually, an underground bunker that could double as a bomb shelter, should that ever prove necessary.

"But you keep telling us that she is the key to expediting our dominance of quantum computing," said a frustrated woman who had already made her fortune in Silicon Valley but was eager to make another one.

"She will be," said Dr. Zimm. "Especially when she starts working with Lenard." He pointed to the robot, who stood silently beside him, blinking and grinning. The pinpoint spotlight directly over his plastic head made his sculpted hair look like the wavy wax pile left behind by a sputtering black candle.

"Ladies and gentlemen," said Dr. Zimm, "believe me when I tell you that, without a doubt, Max Einstein possesses the most brilliant mind in the field of quantum mechanics. Hers is the twenty-first-century brain that will take the leaps Albert Einstein, himself, could not!"

"How do you know that?" demanded the chairman.

Dr. Zimm grinned. "I just do."

Lenard giggled.

"How?" demanded the Russian oligarch on the board. "Have you worked with her before? Did you know her parents? Was she a student of yours?"

"That is my secret to keep."

"Dr. Zimm and Max Einstein have a special connection," said Lenard. "Or, at least, that's what he keeps telling me." Another giggle.

"We want our quantum computer!" shouted the representative of Big Banking. "A closed system that no one else can access without paying us a fee!"

"Of course you do," said Dr. Zimm. "We all do."

Dr. Zimm knew that standard computers, with their bits and bytes, their zeros and ones, could only work on problems one step at a time. Quantum computers, on the other hand, would use the concepts of quantum entanglement and superposition where each zero could be tangled up with a one. The zeros and ones could exist on top of each other. They could be there and not there at the same time.

In other words, quantum computers could work on problems in all sorts of simultaneous steps.

They could solve complex problems much faster than the most sophisticated "classic" computer.

They would be worth a lot more money.

"In time," Dr. Zimm told the board, "Max Einstein will see that she is better off with us. With *me*."

"That's what you keep telling us," said the woman from Big Media, her anger rising. "But we're in a race, doctor. We're not the only ones working on quantum computing. Microsoft, Google, IBM, Caltech, MIT—they're all chasing after the same prize!"

"But none of them have Max Einstein!" shouted Dr. Zimm.

"Neither do we!" the chairman shouted back.

"But we will," said Lenard, a smile creeping across his rubbery face. "I am, at this very moment, cross-referencing several intelligence sources and social media feeds that will, I can say with ninety-six percent certainty, tell us where we might apprehend Maxine. However, at this instant, my computations are only operating at thirty-three percent of their potential capacity. I am having trouble linking to the external cellular network. Perhaps you should reconsider your decision to locate your headquarters in an underground bunker? Either that, or install better Wi-Fi."

He giggled.

The board was stunned into silence. Dr. Zimm, too.

"What about Dr. Zimm?" said the chairman, directing his question to Lenard. "If we have *you* to grab the girl, why do we need *him*?"

"Good question," said Lenard. "However, in my estimation, Dr. Zimm remains a useful, if non-vital, element in our equation for success because of his claim of a special relationship with our target. However, going forward, I assure you that I will be leading the hunt for Maxine Einstein. I also assure you that she will be in Corp custody soon. Very soon."

And then he giggled and chuckled. For a full minute and a half.

22

When Max and her team landed in Galway they were greeted at the airport by someone they hadn't expected to bump into in Ireland.

Klaus, the blustery, sausage-loving, CMI robotics expert from Poland.

"Are you here to carry our bags?" asked Siobhan.

"Nope," said Klaus, puffing up his chest. "Got a call from the benefactor. You know, the guy in charge of this whole CMI thing."

"Ben called you?" said Max.

"Yeah. Said you guys might need my help. So I dropped everything and caught the first plane I could—and believe me, I was quite busy back home, building some amazing robots that do incredible things. I brought a few with me."

He jabbed a pudgy thumb over his shoulder to indicate several large wooden crates.

"Gonna need some help transporting my gear, Charl. Maybe you and Isabl could organize a truck for us?"

Charl glared at Klaus. "Ben told you to fly here?"

"Of course he did," said Klaus. "Why else do you think I'm here?"

Max was confused. Ben hadn't mentioned summoning Klaus to Ireland during their dinner together back on Long Island. *And why did Ben think they needed Klaus?* Didn't he trust Max, Siobhan, and Tisa? Did he think they needed a boy to get this job done? Max sure didn't. She was tempted to give Ben a call. Right away. But she resisted the urge. She could take care of her own problems. She didn't need Ben—the same way she didn't need Klaus.

"I'll check into this," said Isabl, slipping away from the group, thumbing a speed dial number on her secure satellite phone.

"You should probably look into renting that truck," Klaus said to Charl. "Chop, chop."

Charl squinted at him. Hard. "Wait here, you guys. I'll be right back."

He headed off to the rental counters.

"So what's the plan?" asked Klaus. "Are we putting up some more solar panels?"

"No," said Max.

"We're here to help Siobhan," said Tisa.

"Oh, right," said Klaus. "That thing with the thing. I got your text. Sorry I didn't answer it. Like I said, been busy. Hey, Max—did you get that postcard I sent you in New York?"

"Yes."

"The offer still stands. You want to take a break? Stand down from the pressure of being team leader? If so, I'm definitely ready to step up."

"This isn't an official CMI project," Max explained. "Although Ben will be financing our efforts, we're only here to help Siobhan figure out why so many of her friends, neighbors, and family are getting sick."

Isabl rejoined the group. "Klaus's story checks out. Ben wants him here. Thinks we might need some robotic assistance."

"Hey," said Siobhan, "me and my family will take all the assistance we can get. Human and not-so-human."

"Are you talking about Klaus or his robots?" cracked Tisa.

"Cute, Tisa," said Klaus. "Cute."

Fifteen minutes later, the team was loading their suitcases and Klaus's robot crates into the back of a rented Mercedes van with room for six passengers and cargo.

"My folks are in Terelicken," said Siobhan, "just outside Ballymahon."

"The GPS says it's a little more than an hour away if we take the M6," said Isabl, who, of course, was behind the wheel of the van.

"Can we stop for lunch along the way?" asked Klaus. "I'm starving. Can you hear my stomach gurgling? I can."

"I know a good fish n' chips shop on a road right outside Galway," said Siobhan.

When they entered the roadside restaurant, Max learned something new: "chips" are what people in Ireland call French fries (while they call potato chips "crisps"). As they waited for their food, Klaus started suggesting all sorts of solutions to problems in Terelicken and Ballymahon.

"It's a water problem, right? What if we worked out a deal with a bottled water distributor? If the benefactor is going to pay for everything, he could pay to have clean water delivered."

"That's not a sustainable solution," said Tisa, splashing malted vinegar on her fried fish because that's what Siobhan was doing with hers.

"Well," said Klaus, "some eggheads down at Bristol University in the UK have invented something they call the row-bot. Put it in a river or lake and it can clean up pollution and generate electricity from it at the same time!

The secret is a microbial fuel cell that digests the bacteria in the water and produces electrons that can be used to row its oars so it can paddle around looking for more food—also known as pollution—to gobble down. It doesn't need any kind of external energy. It's completely self-sufficient. Sort of like me."

"We're not dealing with a polluted river or lake," said Siobhan.

"Okay. How about we build a robot to—"

"How about we assess the problem first?" suggested Tisa.

"I agree," said Max.

"And so would Einstein!" exclaimed Siobhan. "Didn't he say, 'If I had an hour to solve a problem, I'd spend fifty-five minutes thinking about the problem and five minutes thinking about solutions'?"

"Well," said Max. "There's no evidence that Albert Einstein ever said that, although a lot of people attribute that quote to him online. But! I do think he'd agree with the sentiment."

And, she thought, *even Albert Einstein might need to spend even* more *time thinking about the problem if that problem's name was Klaus.*

23

When Max and her team arrived at Siobhan's home in the Irish midlands, her younger brother, Séamus, was still sick in bed.

"So are a lot of other people who live outside of town like we do," said Siobhan's mother, Mrs. McKenna. "The Dowdalls, who are both quite old. The little Morton girls. The Rourkes, the Bannons, and the Muldoons. They all have someone down with stomach cramps or worse."

"And they all live outside the town of Ballymahon?" asked Max.

"Aye, that they do."

"And we all get our water from wells," said Siobhan.

"Boom!" said Klaus. "That's your problem, folks. You need to build a new water supply system. Maybe a dam.

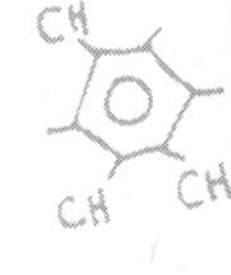

Aqueducts. Water purification facilities. We'll need pipes. Lots and lots of water pipes."

Mrs. McKenna raised her eyebrows. "Is this the sausage-loving boy you told me about?" she asked Siobhan.

"Aye."

"Well, why don't you come with me, lad? You ever try Winston's Irish Style Bangers?"

"No, ma'am."

Mrs. McKenna led Klaus toward the kitchen.

"Oh, they're quite lovely, indeed. We'll serve it up with onion stout gravy, mashed potatoes, and peas...."

"Thank you, Mam," whispered Siobhan when Klaus was out of the room.

"We should definitely sample your well water, Siobhan," said Tisa, the biochemist. "We'll be looking for coliform bacteria, which, of course, are present in the feces of animals and humans."

"Nice," said Siobhan, sarcastically.

"Those bacteria don't cause illness, but their presence in drinking water is an indication that the water is contaminated with sewage." Tisa opened one of her rolling suitcases. "I brought along several bacteria testing kits. I never leave home without my chemistry set."

"Where's the well head?" asked Max.

"Around back," said Siobhan. "Come on."

Max followed Siobhan and Tisa out the back door and into the barnyard. The McKennas were potato farmers. Siobhan had four brothers and three sisters. Most of them were bustling around the homestead, doing chores, pitching in, making each other laugh.

"So these are the two lassies with brains even bigger than yours?" joked Siobhan's father when he met them at the well head.

"Aye," said Siobhan. "Da, meet Max and Tisa."

"Thank you both for coming all this way to lend a hand," said Mr. McKenna. "Now then, let's open up this well and do some serious scientific research, eh? Of course, this part of the job needs a wee bit more brawn than brains. Aidan? Get over here and give your poor old Da a hand."

While Mr. McKenna and Siobhan's older brother Aidan wrenched open the well cap (with some help from another brother named Quinn), Max couldn't help but feel happy.

And sad.

This was the kind of big family she'd always dreamed about belonging to. But she had no parents. No brothers or sisters. No one like Siobhan who was willing to drop everything and fly halfway around the world to get her help.

That's why, even though she'd never admit it to her

CMI friends, Max was secretly intrigued by the mysterious Dr. Zimm. When they met in the Congo, he'd told her: "I know who you are. I know where you came from! I know everything you've ever yearned to know!"

Was he telling the truth?

Hard to say. At the time, the creepy mad scientist had been trying to lure Max to climb up a swaying rope ladder into a hovering helicopter.

"Got it," said Tisa, snapping Max out of her thoughts.

Tisa held a small capped vial filled with water the McKennas had siphoned up from the well pipe. "That's all we need to run the test."

"We should collect samples from the wells at any of the homes where there are people with similar gastrointestinal illnesses," suggested Max.

"Too right," said Mr. McKenna. "Come on. I'll drive you about. Introduce you to the neighbors."

"And bring your pipe wrench, Da," said Siobhan. "We might need it."

"You might need me, too," said Aidan, with a wink. "Da's not as strong as he used to be."

"It's true," added Quinn, patting his belly. "He's gone a bit soft...."

"I can still handle you lot!" said Mr. McKenna, with a hearty laugh.

And so, after a brief wrestling match, the three McKenna men joined Max, Tisa, and Siobhan as they set out to test water at six other wells.

By sundown, they'd gathered their samples.

By midnight, they knew what was causing all the trouble.

24

"It's *E. coli,*" announced Tisa. "Short for *Escherichia*
coli. This is a particularly ugly strain. *E. coli* O157:H7."

Both Max and Siobhan nodded.

They were dealing with a nasty type of fecal coliform bacteria. Although most strains were harmless and lived inside the intestines of healthy humans and animals, this particular strain produced a powerful toxin that could cause severe illness.

"This is a very strong indication of sewage or animal waste contamination," said Tisa.

"The sheep," mumbled Siobhan.

"What do you mean?" asked Max.

"There are all sorts of sheep herds on farms up in the neighboring hills. I reckon sheep poop has been washing

downhill every time it rains and this unpleasant bacteria has been seeping down into our water table."

"We should go on a field trip," suggested Max. "First thing in the morning. See if there's a way to easily redirect the runoff."

"Or," said Siobhan, "maybe we can ask the sheep to kindly stop pooping!"

The friends laughed.

Klaus came into the room. "What's so funny?" he asked with a burp. "Did I miss something?"

"Yes," said Siobhan. "Everything!"

In the morning, Charl and Isabl drove the four-member CMI crew up into the hills surrounding the McKenna farm.

"Mr. McGregor has a rather large flock," said Siobhan. "About two hundred ewes."

"Hey," said Klaus, "there's only one me."

Everybody else just rolled their eyes.

As Isabl piloted the rumbling van up the rutted road leading to the McGregors' farmhouse, Klaus wrestled open a crate in the cargo bay.

"We'll go inside, talk to the McGregors," said Charl. "Let them know what you're up to on their land."

"Thanks," said Max. "Come on, guys."

"I'll be out in a minute," said Klaus, rummaging through one of his wooden boxes. "I have an idea. . . ."

"Saints preserve us," muttered Siobhan.

She, Tisa, and Max went to the crest of an emerald-green hill where sheep were grazing on both sides. They were all glad that the McKennas had lent them rubber stable mucker boots. There were mounds and pellets of sheep dung everywhere they stepped.

"Our place is down that way," said Siobhan, indicating the western horizon.

Tisa pointed to the ground. "So, bacteria from *that* might be in your well water a few months from now."

"Where's the McGregors' well?" asked Max.

"I reckon over there," said Siobhan, pointing at a cast-iron hand pump in front of the barn.

"We should go grab a sample of their water," Max suggested. "It'd be interesting if their water is tainted, too. Cooperation in this project might prove to be its key."

Max was remembering something her idol once said: "Nothing truly valuable can be achieved except by the unselfish cooperation of many individuals." She realized it would be great if the McGregors were some of those individuals unselfishly cooperating.

As the three friends hurried over to the well to pump a water sample, they heard an annoying, high-pitched

High-tech.

Low-tech.

Same solution.

chorus of whines behind them. The whirring hum was soon accompanied by the raucous braying of startled sheep.

"That fool eejit!" shouted Siobhan.

Klaus had sent a robotic drone flying at the sheep grazing on the downhill slope. He was using the four-propellered hovering robot like a border collie to chase the frightened flock up the hill.

"Problem solved!" Klaus shouted as he thumbed the drone's remote controls. "The sheep will no longer poop on Siobhan's side of the hill! Your well water is saved!"

Suddenly, a shotgun blasted.

And Klaus's plastic drone exploded in midair before chunks of it fell to the ground with a barrage of thuds—like a flock of geese that'd just forgotten how to fly.

25

"Did you get what you need?" Max asked Tisa as the buckshot blast echoed like thunder around the hills and knolls.

"Yes," said Tisa, capping her water sample vial.

"Get off my farm, you little brats!" shouted a farmer, who Max assumed was Mr. McGregor. He was toting a smoldering shotgun and had just cracked open its breech to reload. Charl and Isabl came running out of the farmhouse after him.

"Everyone!" shouted Isabl, running toward the parked van. "Get into the vehicle. Now!"

"We're leaving, sir," Max heard Charl tell the farmer. "We meant no harm."

"That idiot boy with the X-Box scared my sheep half to death!"

"It's not an X-Box," shouted Klaus, as he ran toward the van. "It's the remote control for the Phantom Four Pro V 2.0 drone you just shot down, which, by the way, cost me more than thirteen hundred euros!"

"How much is it going to cost to have a doctor remove the buckshot pellets I'm gonna pepper in your pants, boyo?" asked the farmer, waving his shotgun.

"Klaus?" shouted Charl. "Into the van, now. Mr. McGregor? Kindly lower your weapon."

The way Charl said it sounded as if the farmer would be the one with serious wounds if he disobeyed.

Klaus, Max, Siobhan, and Tisa hustled into the van, where Isabl already had the motor revving. Charl tapped the roof as he swung into the passenger seat.

"Go!"

Tires squealed. Pebbles spewed. Isabl executed an amazingly tight U-turn and, as fast as she could fly without lifting off the ground, put some distance between the van's rear bumper and farmer McGregor's shotgun.

"I thought it was a good idea," said Klaus, after the farm disappeared in the distance.

"Seriously?" said Siobhan.

"Yes!" said Klaus, defensively. "If the sheep stay on the other side of the hill, your well water will stay safe."

"But," said Tisa, "you automatically double the pollution probability for any families downhill on the other side."

"Herding sheep is an old solution," said Max, "no matter how you dress it up with robots. We need to look at this problem differently. We need to use our imaginations."

Max knew that logic would get you from point A to point B. But imagination could take you anywhere.

The team returned to their makeshift lab in the root cellar of Siobhan's house. Except Klaus. He went back to the kitchen to sample more Irish food.

"He's not much of a team player," said Tisa.

"Ah, he just needs to pout," said Siobhan. "Besides, we three are better off without him."

"His heart was in the right place," said Max.

"Maybe," said Siobhan. "Too bad his brain was in his butt."

"Mr. McGregor's well water is contaminated, too," said Tisa after running her *E. coli* analysis.

"Confirming that redirecting the runoff isn't really the solution to our bigger problem," said Max.

"Then what is?" asked Siobhan.

"Not sure. Excuse me."

"Where are you going?"

"Out back. I want to spend some time with your well."

"Really?"

"Yeah."

And so Max did what she thought Dr. Einstein would've done: She stood in the yard. For hours. Staring at the rusty pipe sticking up out of the green grass and clover.

She wasn't used to this kind of pressure. People were counting on her. Friends. Their sick families. Would she let them all down?

She ran a thought experiment in her head, assisted by that imagined voice of Einstein she liked to talk to whenever she had to wrangle a problem into a solution.

"So," said her internal Einstein, "how does the *E. coli* get into the well water?"

"It seeps into the ground," Max silently replied. "Whenever it rains, the water becomes polluted by animal waste."

"Yes, that is how the bacteria gets into the water. But, Maxine, you have not addressed the fundamental issue in my question. How does the *E. coli* get into the *well* water?"

"Okay," said Max. "Coliform bacteria that gets washed into the ground by rain is usually filtered out as the water goes through the soil and into groundwater systems."

"Exactly. But what if that natural filtration is not

enough? What if a well is poorly constructed, cracked, or unsealed?"

"Of course! The wells are the problem, not the water. We need to disinfect them. . . ."

"Yes," said her mental Einstein. "Might I suggest Cl_2? Chlorine?"

"We could use chlorine bleach. Then we need to test all the well seals and fix any cracked casings."

Max pulled out a small, battered notebook and started jotting down notes, sketching ideas. They'd need to go through the affected area with a two-step approach. Disinfecting all the wells, then repairing any fissures or cracks in the well linings and casings.

They'd need to first scrub and chemically disinfect the pipes burrowing down into the earth.

In dozens, maybe hundreds of wells. Which could take a very long time.

Unless . . .

Max grinned.

She hurried inside.

"Klaus?" she yelled into the kitchen. "Put down that sausage. We need a new robot. Now!"

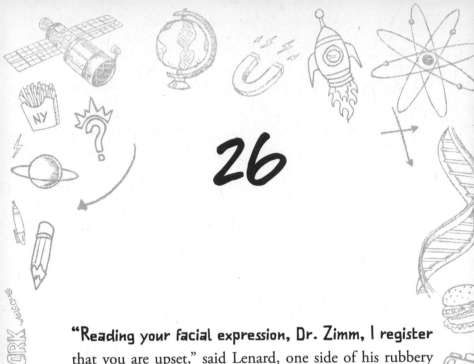

26

"Reading your facial expression, Dr. Zimm, I register that you are upset," said Lenard, one side of his rubbery lips curling up into the semblance of a sinister grin. "Why? Has your human intelligence failed you? Again?"

"My undercover contact usually reports on a regular basis," said Dr. Zimm. "I haven't had a message in nearly a week."

"I know. You see, doctor, I have full access to all your accounts. E-mail, texts, Twitter, Instagram, Snapchat. You really should spend more time thinking about your passwords. And you should not be so consistent in your use of the same eight-digit string of letters, numbers, and an exclamation point. You should make this game more challenging for me."

"We need to find Max Einstein!" Dr. Zimm pounded his fist on the table, rattling the three-level chessboard set up between him and his humanoid helper. *Or was Lenard the boss, now?* That's what his artificially intelligent cohort had declared inside the Corp boardroom. And the board members hadn't disagreed.

A few chess pieces toppled to the floor.

"Is that your move, Dr. Zimm? Rook two and knight three to the floor? Not that it would matter. I am two moves away from checkmating you on levels one and three. One move away on level two. I have surveyed all of your available options and there is no move you can make to stymie my attack. Would you like to surrender now, or should we keep on playing?"

"What we should be doing, Lenard, is finding my informant so they might help us find young Miss Einstein."

Lenard giggled. "What sort of information are you looking for? News? Weather? Sports?"

"Not 'information.' Our informant. Our spy."

"Oh. I have already taken care of that."

"What?"

"As I noted earlier, I have access to all your contacts. Therefore, I know who has been supplying you with data about Max Einstein's whereabouts. Her dwelling place above the stables in New York City, for instance. I have traced the whereabouts of your unwitting traitor... your unsuspecting spy...what is the proper or preferred terminology?"

"Informant!"

"Thank you. I have traced the whereabouts of your informant's cell phone and have located its GPS chip in Ireland. Would you like its exact coordinates?"

"Of course!" said Dr. Zimm, rolling his chair over to his computer and clacking keys to call up Google maps. "Okay. I'm ready. Tell me."

"I find speaking to be an enjoyable but inefficient means of relaying data. I have already entered the IP address for your preferred mapping application into your computer's random-access memory. You should be looking at a map of the rural area surrounding Ballymahon on the River Inny. The most recent population data suggests 2,674 people live there." Another giggle. "That survey did not include your informant and their friends."

"What friends?"

"I suspect several members of the Change Makers Institute are there now. As you may not be aware, since you have not undertaken the deep data dive that I recently completed, a potato farm on the outskirts of Ballymahon is where Siobhan McKenna lives with her family."

"Who?"

"Siobhan McKenna. She is a young geoscientist whom you previously met in Africa."

"She's one of the genius children on Max Einstein's team?"

"Correct. Cross-referencing the geographic location of your informant with current events as described on the *Longford Leader* website..."

"The Longford who?"

"The local Irish newspaper. They cover Ballymahon and the surrounding area. Shall I continue?"

"Yes."

"Several farming families in the area have been experiencing gastrointestinal illnesses. In such instances, well water is often considered the culprit."

"So," said Dr. Zimm, stroking his tiny chin, "there's a public health problem in need of a solution."

"Correct. Responding to such a humanitarian crisis, particularly as it might involve friends and family of one of its members, would match the 'do-gooder' profile of the Change Makers Institute and its team of young scientists."

Now Dr. Zimm had a grin on his face almost as creepy as the one molded into Lenard's artificial face.

"Well, bless their young hearts for all the good work they do around the globe," he said sarcastically. "It makes them so much easier to hunt down."

27

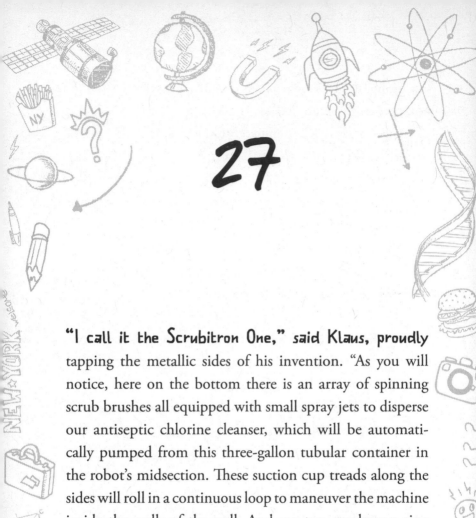

"I call it the Scrubitron One," said Klaus, proudly tapping the metallic sides of his invention. "As you will notice, here on the bottom there is an array of spinning scrub brushes all equipped with small spray jets to disperse our antiseptic chlorine cleanser, which will be automatically pumped from this three-gallon tubular container in the robot's midsection. These suction cup treads along the sides will roll in a continuous loop to maneuver the machine inside the walls of the well. And, up top, we have a ring of night-vision cameras providing a three-hundred-and-sixty-degree view that will tell these two dozen miniature caulking arms where to apply their sealant. Think of the Scrubitron One as a robotic well-cleaning-and-repairing

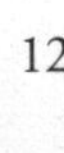

submarine, fully equipped to do the entire anti–*E. coli* job in one fell swoop!"

"It looks like an upside-down squid," said Tisa.

"It looks like it'll get the job done," said Max with a smile.

"It looks absolutely amazing!" said Siobhan. Then she surprised Klaus (and probably herself) by throwing her arms around his neck and kissing him on the cheek. "You are a bloomin' genius!"

"Um, thanks," said Klaus, momentarily stunned out of his usual bluster. "I guess we all are."

"Which is why I wanted to work with you guys instead of the adult scientists they tried to saddle me with after we did all that testing in Jerusalem to find a team leader," said Max.

"You think the benefactor made a mistake?" Klaus said to Siobhan. "You think billionaire Ben should've picked me to lead the team?" His bluster was back. His swagger, too.

"Nah," said Siobhan. "I think I'm the only one who made a mistake. I misjudged you, Klaus. I thought you were nothin' but an overgrown child playing with all your electronic toys and gizmos. Turns out you're a top notch AI and robotics wizard."

It had only taken Klaus a day to develop and build his "Scrubitron One" after Max gave him the challenge (and the benefactor gave him a credit card to go buy anything he needed to build his bot). He'd come through for the team, big time. All that was left was to field test his clever device.

"We'll send it down your well, first," Max said to Siobhan.

"If it flops," said Tisa, "nobody else has to know."

"It's not going to flop!" said Klaus. "It's going to be brilliant. Believe me."

The McKenna family (mom, dad, brothers, sisters, aunts, uncles, cousins, and assorted dogs) gathered around the well as Max and her team fed the self-contained scrubbing/sealing machine down the dark pipe.

It took the bot two hours to clean, disinfect, and repair the well.

"It could've taken longer," Klaus told Siobhan's father, "but your well casing was in pretty good shape, sir." He shared a screenshot from his tablet computer where he had recorded and monitored what the robot's night-vision cameras had seen below. "But you did have a significant fissure at about fifteen feet down. That could be where the nasty little sheep poop microbes snuck into your water."

Tisa tested samples of water from the well at regular intervals throughout the day.

"The *E. coli* numbers have dropped dramatically," she reported after dinner.

"How dramatically?" asked Siobhan.

Tisa grinned. "It's all gone. Your water is sparkling clean again."

This time Siobhan hugged Tisa. Then, for good measure, she hugged Max and Klaus, too.

"My family and I can't ever thank you three enough," she said, her eyes watering up. "Now look what you've done. You made me all weepy. I don't do weepy."

They spent the next day using Klaus's ingenious invention to clean and seal wells at neighboring farms.

Near dusk, they went back to the McGregors', where hundreds of sheep were out in the hilly fields grazing.

"Your water is contaminated, sir," Max told Mr. McGregor. "We ran a test and—"

"Is that what's making my little girl sick?"

"We think so, sir."

"Can you fix it?"

Max nodded. "We just need to send a robot down your well."

Klaus, who, of course, remembered the shotgun blast that took down his drone, stood at the back of the van, protectively cradling the Scrubitron in his arms.

"Thank you," said the sheep herder. "But can I ask a wee favor?"

"Sure," said Max.

"Keep that bloomin' robot away from my sheep!"

28

After two dozen wells were sanitized and sealed, and Siobhan's little brother, Séamus, was feeling better, the neighbors decided to host a party to celebrate the "young brainy ones" and to say thanks.

"They're throwin' a bash for us this Friday night at Leavy's of Foigha," said Siobhan. "It's a pub and grocery store combined. Should be good fun. Lots of music, dancin', and food. All the folks we helped will be there—and the ones whose wells we haven't gotten to yet. Séamus will be comin', too!"

On Friday night, Charl and Isabl drove Max, Tisa, and Klaus the three kilometers from the McKenna home near Terelicken to Leavy's of Foigha. Siobhan rode with her family.

"I'll stay with the vehicle," Isabl announced as they pulled into a parking spot.

"Why?" said Klaus.

"It's standard protocol when you guys are in an unsecured public area," Isabl explained. "We might need to leave here in a hurry."

"Why?" said Klaus. "Is the food going to be bad?"

"It's a bloomin' party, Isabl," Siobhan protested. "People are comin' to have fun, not to cause trouble."

Isabl smiled. "Let's hope so."

Klaus rolled his eyes. "Party pooper."

"I'll be inside with you guys," said Charl.

"We'll bring you out a plate of food," Max promised Isabl.

"Thank you."

When Max and her friends stepped into the pub, they couldn't believe how packed the place was. Everyone gave them a round of applause.

"Thank you, you brilliant lads and lasses!" shouted the farmer, Mr. McGregor, raising a glass of dark-amber liquid that Max figured was probably Irish whiskey. The strong stuff. Eighty proof, which meant that 40 percent of the liquid in the glass was alcohol and, therefore, extremely flammable. That might explain Mr. McGregor's bright-red nose. "Here's to you and your robots!"

He raised his glass and so did all the other adults in the pub.

"May the roof above us never fall in," cried Mr. McGregor, making a toast. "And may we friends gathered below never fall out!"

"Hear, hear!" shouted the crowd.

Then someone turned on the jukebox. First came a dance tune played on Irish hornpipes. That was followed by a slew of Motown oldies that everybody sang along with. Kids, some of whom had been sick in bed a few days earlier (including Séamus), were playing hide-and-seek behind the barstools and grocery store racks. Platters of food—piled high with shepherd's pie, herbed beef pastries, bowls of beef stew, corned beef and cabbage sliders, and lemon curd sponge cake—were passed around.

"You need any help in the kitchen?" Tisa asked the man behind the bar who seemed to be in charge of all the food and drink.

"We can always use an extra hand," he told her.

"Good. I love cooking and baking. It's like doing chemistry you can eat!"

"I love eating," said Klaus, stuffing another meat pie in his face.

Max laughed and felt a blast of hot air as the pub doors swung open.

Three men in black suits had just entered the bar. They were accompanied by someone Max recognized immediately.

Dr. Zimm.

The crowd grew quiet. Someone shut off the jukebox. No one but the CMI team knew who the surly, uninvited guests might be.

"What's that clacking contraption behind you?" cried Mr. McGregor from his perch at the bar. "Another one of Klaus's robots? I must say, he's a far sight better-looking than that thing we sent down the wells."

Max finally saw what the farmer had already seen. A humanoid sculpted to resemble a smirking thirteen-year-old boy. Its face was creepily lifelike. Its movements herky-jerky and jagged.

"Hello, Max," said Dr. Zimm. "It's so good to sec you again."

Charl stepped forward, his hand moving to the holster strapped to his hip.

The boy-bot's eyes scanned the security leader's face with a green laser grid.

"I would not do that, Charl," it said. "The three gentlemen who escorted us into this establishment are also carrying weapons. Triangulating their projected trajectories, I can predict, with ninety-eight percent certitude, that you

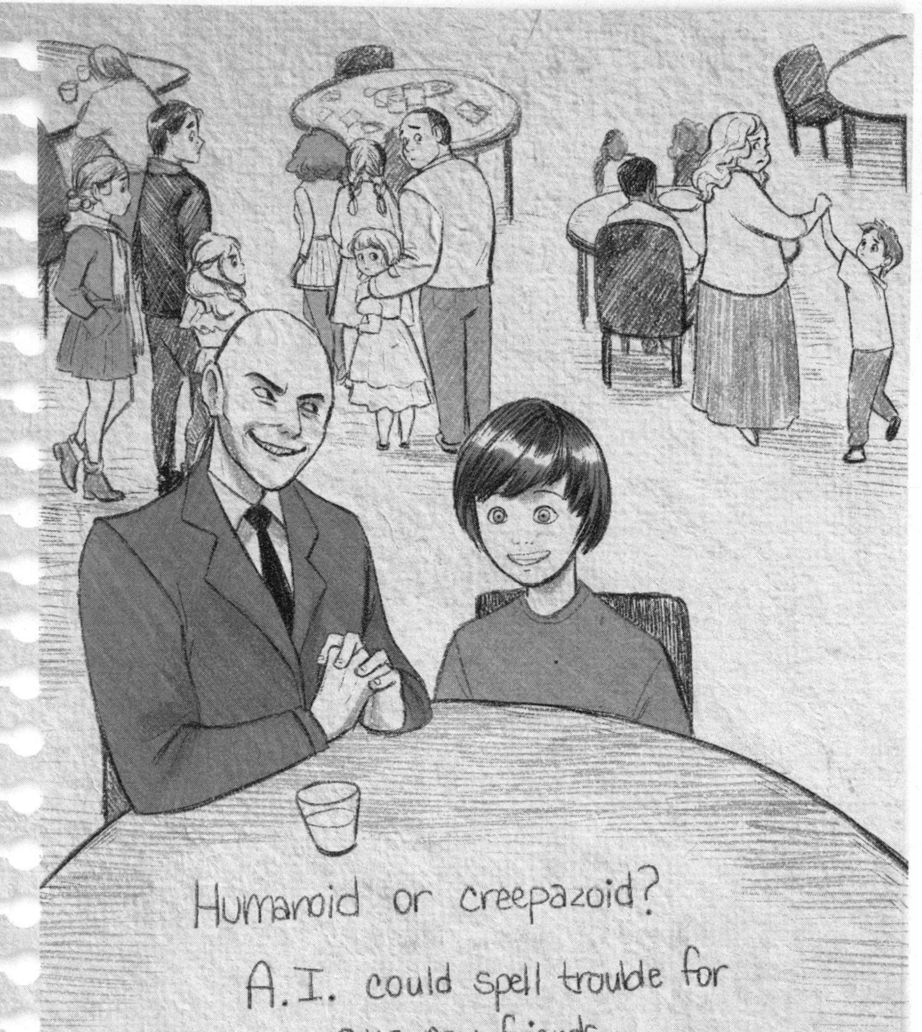

Humanoid or creepazoid?

A.I. could spell trouble for our new friends.

I agree with his projections: We are in big trouble.

might be able to injure one of my humans but there would be much more collateral damage on your side, including the death of innocent bystanders. I project at least five. Maybe more. Including several children and infants." Now the robot sniggered.

"How'd you know my name?" demanded Charl.

"The same way he knew how to find Max," gloated Dr. Zimm. "Lenard is brilliant. But not nearly as bright as you, Maxine. Which is why I know you are about to make a very wise decision."

"Oh, really?" said Max. "And what might that be?"

"To come work with us."

"It would be fun," added Lenard. "Unlike Dr. Zimm, you might actually be able to defeat me in chess."

And then, of course, he giggled.

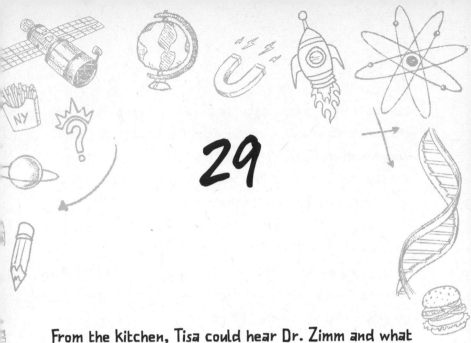

29

From the kitchen, Tisa could hear Dr. Zimm and what sounded like a robotic young boy.

"We would've arrived sooner," said Dr. Zimm. "But, well, there is so much bureaucracy when you work for a large corporation. Forms to fill out. Expense requisitions..."

"You have sixty seconds to make your decision, Max," chirped the high-pitched boy-bot.

Tisa grabbed a pair of rubber dishwashing gloves and started scrounging through the pantry shelves as quietly as she could. She found what she was looking for: baking soda, vinegar, and, most important, a spice bottle full of red pepper.

* * *

"Come with us, Max," said Dr. Zimm. "We have no interest in your friends. They can go back to cleaning wells. You, however, are destined for far greater things."

"We're going to build a quantum computer together," said the humanoid. "Won't that be fun?"

"Stand back, you lot," said Mr. McGregor. "You make a move for the girl and—"

"And what?" said the robot. "Are you forgetting that you are outgunned and in a no-win situation? Do I need to run my statistical analysis for you again?"

"No need," said Max. "Mr. McGregor? Why don't you pour our guests some of that Irish whiskey you've been drinking? It's 80 proof, right?"

"No, lassie. This is Redbreast. It's *115* proof."

Max did the math. Divide by two. The whiskey was 57.5 percent alcohol. It was perfect.

"Then pour Dr. Zimm and his friends a glass. Except the robot. You don't drink, do you, Lenard?"

"No," Lenard said with a giggle. "Ingesting liquids is bad for my circuitry."

"Max?" called Tisa from the kitchen. "I have something I'd like to give our guests, too."

"Perfect," Max hollered back to the kitchen. "And don't

forget to light a candle and stick it in a meat pie. It's Klaus's birthday."

Klaus had an "it is?" expression on his face until the look on Max's face told him to play along.

"A birthday meat pie would be lovely," said Klaus.

"Dr. Zimm?" said Lenard. "I can only assume that Max and her friends are stalling. Attempting to delay our inevitable victory and departure. It is not Klaus's birthday. As you recall, that was last month."

"But we weren't all together last month," said Max. "This is a belated birthday celebration. I just need to see Klaus blow out his candle, then I'm ready to roll out of here with you guys."

"I've got your drinks, lads," said Mr. McGregor, holding a silver tray with four tumbler glasses filled to the rim with amber whiskey.

The three Corp goons looked to Dr. Zimm.

"A quick drink will be fine, gentlemen," said Dr. Zimm. "After all, now that Max has agreed to leave with us, we have much to celebrate. The future. Redeeming Dr. Einstein's mistakes about quantum physics. You are his true heir, Max. You can take the theory the great Einstein couldn't quite grasp and bring it to life!"

"Works for me," said Max, who really was trying to buy some time.

Finally, Tisa and a cook came out of the kitchen.

Tisa was holding a rubber glove that jiggled like a water balloon. The glove had been inflated so much its fingers were extended. The thing looked like a bloated cow udder. The cook carried a plate with a meat pie spiked with half a dozen flickering birthday candles.

"Happy birthday to me," Klaus sang loudly and off key. "Happy birthday to me!"

While everyone was distracted by his squawking (and covering their ears), Tisa dashed forward and pulled out a paring knife. She poked a series of holes in the bulging fingertips of her inflated glove. The carbon dioxide gas created when she combined baking soda with vinegar came spewing out of the openings, like warm soda shooting out of a shaken can. That gas carried with it the flecks of red pepper. Tisa aimed her improvised tear gas straight into the trio of armed thugs' eyes.

Meanwhile, Max plucked a candle out of the birthday pie and tossed it into one of the whiskey glasses on Mr. McGregor's tray. The alcohol erupted into blue flames. Mr. McGregor flipped the serving platter like a catapult and doused Lenard with the fiery liquid.

"Unacceptable," squeaked Lenard as flames licked up his chest and singed his plastic face. "Unacceptable!"

Dr. Zimm grabbed a nearby tablecloth and tried to blot

out the fire, which had already melted one of Lenard's eyebrows into a drooping squint.

"Go!" shouted Charl.

The armed men from the Corp were still blinded by Tisa's red-pepper tear gas and couldn't find their weapons.

Siobhan, Tisa, Max, and Klaus raced out the pub door and practically threw themselves into Isabl's waiting van. Charl tumbled into the passenger seat five seconds after everyone else was safely on board.

"Initiate extraction package," Charl told Isabl.

She jammed her foot down on the accelerator. The van blasted off.

"Good job in there, Tisa and Max," said Charl.

"What about the townspeople?" asked Max.

"Dr. Zimm isn't interested in them. He'll be chasing after us—just as soon as his men can see straight and his robot isn't melting. You guys bought us at least a sixty-second head start."

And with the way Isabl was driving?

Sixty seconds might be all they needed.

30

A few miles away from the pub, Isabl screeched to a stop on the shoulder of the road, pulling in behind a parked tractor trailer.

"That's our next ride," said Charl.

"You can drive the big rig, Charl," said Isabl. "I'll stay here with the team."

"Roger that. Let me go open the loading gate."

He hurried out of the van and pressed a boxy button on the side of the truck. Its rear door rolled up while a ramp extended from a slot above the bumper.

"Seat belts buckled?" said Isabl when the nose of the ramp touched the roadway in front of her tires.

"Yes," said Max. "Always."

Especially with the way Isabl drove.

"Good," said Isabl. She tapped the gas and the van scooted up the ramp and into the empty cargo bay of the truck. Max heard the rear door rumble shut behind them. Seconds later, her whole world lurched forward. The tractor trailer rig was rumbling up the highway with the van hidden inside.

"How'd you two know we'd need a getaway plan like this?" asked Siobhan.

"We didn't *know,*" said Isabl. "But we do try to plan ahead for any contingency. All part of our standard security protocols."

"Because you guys are geniuses, too!" said Max.

Isabl laughed. "We're nowhere near as smart and clever as you kids. But at least Dr. Zimm and his cronies will be searching the roads for a rental van, not an eighteen-wheeler hauling frozen fish for Rockabill Seafood Limited."

An hour or so later, the truck pulled to a stop.

"Where are we?" asked Klaus.

"Safe," said Isabl.

"I meant, what's our location?"

"That, my friend, is currently confidential."

Max heard the cargo door roll up.

"Everybody out," said Isabl. "This concludes the land portion of our travels for today."

Escape from
Ireland
Isabl's Big (Rig)
Disappearing Act

Max and the others marched down the ramp to discover that they were parked beside another remote airstrip. In a green field. Somewhere in Ireland. (Well, that's what she assumed because she didn't think the truck had pulled onto a ferry boat and sailed off the island.) Max didn't have a clue as to where they were because, riding inside the cargo hold of a tractor trailer, she hadn't seen any landmarks or road signs.

Ben's private jet was parked on the tarmac of the secluded airport. A pilot and copilot team were standing by in the cockpit.

"Max?" said Charl. "You and Klaus will be flying on to the next, official CMI project."

"We have a mission?" said Max, eagerly.

Charl nodded. "Ben approved the plan yesterday."

"Siobhan and Tisa?" said Isabl. "We'd like you two to stay here and finish cleaning and repairing the wells."

"With *my* robot?" said Klaus.

"Exactly," said Isabl.

"But—"

"Thanks for making it so user friendly," said Siobhan, clapping Klaus on the back. "I've watched you work it down the pipes for a week now. I'm ready to give it a whirl."

"Mr. McGregor and the local police will be your security detail," Charl said to Tisa and Siobhan. "Isabl and I will be flying on with Max and Klaus. When you complete the well project here, you'll join the rest of the team at the new site."

"Where are we going?" asked Max.

"That information is classified until we are airborne," said Isabl.

"And everyone else will be there?"

Isabl nodded. "Yes. Annika, Keeto, Toma, Hana, and Vihaan have all made travel arrangements. In fact, most of them have already arrived. They'll greet us when we land."

Max felt a fresh rush of adrenaline to replace the one she'd felt back at the pub. This was exciting. She'd be with all her friends again, working on a major project, doing good in a remote corner of the globe—hopefully someplace where Dr. Zimm and his new robot couldn't find them.

"Quick question," said Tisa. "How did Dr. Zimm and the Corp know how to find us?"

"Ben has a theory about an information leak coming out of CMI," said Charl. "Also, that robot, Lenard, is an excellent tracker."

Lenard.

Max wondered if Dr. Zimm was the one who named the artificially intelligent humanoid as a way to goad her. The German experimental physicist Philipp Lenard was one of Albert Einstein's fiercest rivals. As Adolf Hitler gained power before World War II, Lenard argued that Einstein's theories were not "German" enough. Lenard became "Chief of Aryan Physics" under the Nazi regime while Einstein fled in exile to America.

"The Corp's new robot," Charl continued, "operates via artificial intelligence. It knows whatever the Corp has told it. Lenard can also access data from multiple external sources and then sift through it all at a lightning-fast speed."

"So," said Max, "it'll probably only be a matter of time until it figures out where I'm going next."

"Not if we plug the leak," said Isabl. "Artificial intelligence is only as good as the information it is fed."

"Um, exactly what leak are you talking about plugging?" asked Siobhan.

"Ben suspects that someone connected to CMI has been feeding the Corp sensitive information. The Corp, in turn, has been feeding it to Lenard."

"There's a spy?" said Max.

"Maybe," said Charl. "Or it might just be what Vladimir Lenin, the head of Soviet Russia, called a 'useful idiot.' "

"What's that?"

"Someone who helps the enemy without actually knowing they're doing it."

31

Max said good-bye to Tisa and Siobhan.

"Your gear is already stowed on board," Charl told her. "We knew we'd be shipping out sometime tonight after the party. The arrival of Dr. Zimm just accelerated our schedule. The pilots collected all your belongings from Siobhan's house."

"They put my suitcase on the plane?" asked Max.

"Yes," said Isabl. "All your souvenirs are safe."

"And you need to add another one," said Siobhan. "I plucked this for you when we were in that sheep meadow."

"Then I showed her how to press and dry it," said Tisa. "We went with the technique of pressing it between two sheets of wax paper in a heavy book—followed by a quick spritz of Mrs. McKenna's hair spray."

"It's a four-leaf clover, Max," said Siobhan. "May it bring you the same sort of luck that found me and my family the day I met you."

"Thank you," said Max, giving each of the girls a tight hug. After all they'd been through together, Siobhan and Tisa felt like sisters to her. Max might've been an orphan, but she was definitely starting to build a family of her own.

"You got anything for me?" asked Klaus.

"No," said Siobhan, "but I'll have my mam send you some of those sausages you love so much once you lot are settled in your new location."

"Awesome!"

The jet door opened and unfolded its staircase.

"Time to head out," Isabl said to Max and Klaus. "I'll need your phones."

"Why?" wondered Max.

"In case Lenard is tracking them," said Charl.

Max and Klaus handed Isabl their phones. She placed them into foil-wrapped, signal-blocking pouches.

"Kind of extreme, don't you think?" said Klaus.

"Not if there's a leak," said Max.

Klaus shrugged. "Whatever. Be careful with that," he told Isabl as she slid his phone into an aluminum sleeve. "It's brand new."

Mr. McGregor and a police officer from the village arrived to pick up Siobhan and Tisa.

Klaus, Isabl, Charl, and Max climbed aboard the small jet and strapped themselves into their seats. Max waved good-bye through her window to Siobhan and Tisa. As the jet lifted off, she also silently said "Good-bye" to the lush green landscape of Ireland.

"So where are we flying?" asked Klaus.

Isabl checked her watch. "I'll let you know in an hour."

"How long is the flight going to take?"

"Twelve hours."

"Is there food in the galley?"

Isabl nodded.

"Good. Wake me up when it's time for breakfast."

Klaus fluffed a pillow, pulled up his blanket, and quickly fell asleep.

"You should get some rest, too, Max," suggested Charl.

"I will," she said. But she was too mentally jazzed to nod off like Klaus just did. (He was already snoring.)

First, she hadn't completely processed the encounter with Dr. Zimm and his humanoid helper, Lenard. All that stuff he'd said about "redeeming" Dr. Einstein's quantum physics mistakes. "You are his true heir, Max," he'd said. "You can take the theory the great Einstein couldn't quite grasp and bring it to life!"

While Einstein knew that the math behind quantum mechanics worked, he couldn't accept the weirdness of it. "Quantum mechanics is certainly imposing. But an inner voice tells me that this is not yet the real thing," Einstein wrote to Max Born (one of the fathers of quantum mechanics). "Quantum theory yields much, but it hardly brings us closer to the Old One's secrets. I, in any case, am convinced that He does not play dice with the universe."

Einstein's disagreement was with the fundamental idea that, at the quantum (or atomic) level, nature and the universe are totally random and that events happen by mere chance. He insisted something must be missing—that God wouldn't determine the fate of the world on a random roll of the dice.

He was mistaken, and it was one of the things that left him behind as younger scientists moved forward, focused on this new area of science.

Younger scientists like Max and her CMI teammate, Vihaan, who'd be with Max working on, well, whatever they were going to be working on next.

Vihaan, who was only thirteen, already had a university degree in quantum physics and hoped to, one day, develop a unified theory of everything that would be capable of explaining all physical aspects of the universe.

Klaus started snoring louder.

For some reason, that made Max smile.

In some ways, Klaus was a problem as complex as quantum physics. He could be a braggart and a blowhard while simultaneously being helpful and clever. Max wasn't thrilled, at first, when Klaus mysteriously popped up in Ireland. But, at the end of the day, she was glad he was there. Klaus was the only one who could've taken Max's complicated and convoluted solution for the well water problem and engineered a practical and efficient way of actually making it work.

Klaus was a problem with a solution—if you worked on it long enough.

All of a sudden, Klaus popped up, wide awake.

"I figured it out!" he blurted.

"What?" asked Max.

"Where we're going."

"How?" asked Isabl.

"Easy. The flight tracker on the seat back screens shows us headed East-Southeast. It also notes our airspeed." He tapped the screen.

"I thought you were taking a nap," said Max with a laugh.

"I was. But with one eye and my brain open. Multiply the speed times twelve hours coupled with our flight path and I can estimate that we will be landing somewhere in the Indian subcontinent of Asia."

Max looked to Isabl.

Isabl looked at her watch. Apparently, the hour waiting time was up.

"Correct," she said. "Well done, Klaus."

"India?" said Max. "That's where Vihaan lives."

"Exactly. He needs your help even more than Siobhan did."

32

As the flight continued, Charl and Isabl took Max and Klaus through a PowerPoint presentation.

"Here's your next problem in search of a solution," said Charl.

"Excellent," said Max, eager for an official Change Makers mission.

"Can we watch YouTube on that computer?" asked Klaus. He wasn't quite as eager.

"Klaus?" said Max, arching an eyebrow.

"Fine. We'll YouTube later."

Charl continued his presentation. It was like a briefing out of a *Mission: Impossible* movie.

"We'll be landing at the small Chittaganj Airport near Jitwan, India," said Charl. "It's a hill town in the northern

state of Himachal Pradesh, not far from the Himalaya mountains. They're having a clean water crisis."

"Just like in Ireland," mumbled Max as she focused on the images filling the computer screen.

"But do they have sausages like in Ireland?" asked Klaus.

"A lot of Indians are vegetarians," said Max.

"Oh. Right."

Isabl took over the mission presentation. "Recently, people in Jitwan have had to wait nearly four days to get fresh, drinkable water. They line up with buckets to collect it from tankers. They've had to close schools and tell tourists to stay away."

"The people are frustrated," said Charl. "They live near mountains, not in a desert. But heavy demand, mismanaged water resources, and wild weather patterns thanks to climate change have made it virtually impossible for the people to turn on their taps and expect clean, drinkable water to flow out."

Max thought about how, while living in New York City, she always took a constant stream of water gushing out of faucets for granted. She'd think about that the next time she brushed her teeth. Or flushed a toilet to fool her security guards.

"Water is a basic human need," said Isabl. "When people can't get it, they get mad. Our mission may prove

India Water Crisis =
The Crisis in Terelicken[2].

WATER SAVING TIPS:

Turn off tap while brushing teeth.

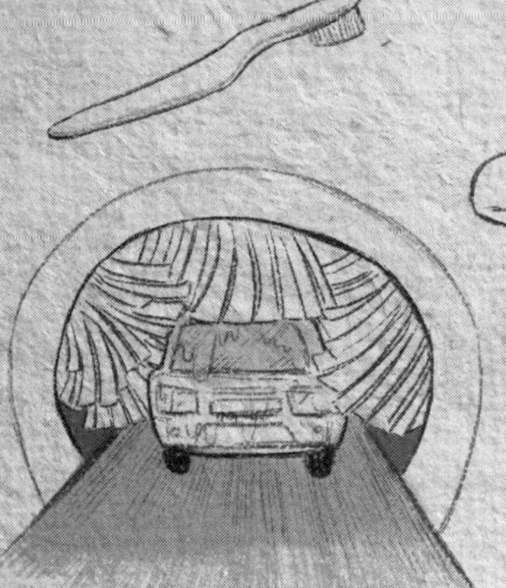

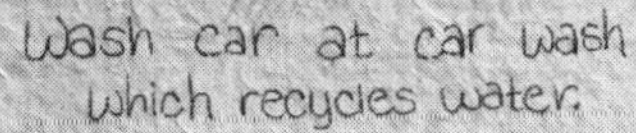

Wash car at car wash which recycles water.

Water plants in the morning.

Shrink the size of your lawn.

dangerous. There have been scattered protests in the streets of Jitwan, even though the government has been hiring contractors to bring in water tankers."

"There has to be a better solution," said Max.

"I don't think so," said Klaus. "Come on. There's a billion people in India and a third of them don't have functioning toilets they can use! They call it 'open defecation.' You know what that means? Outhouses. Ditches. Ducking behind a shrub. There's raw human sewage everywhere! This mission isn't just impossible, it's hopeless!"

Max looked out the window at the snowcapped mountains below. The earth had so much water. The trick was getting it to the right places at the right times and making sure it was clean when it arrived.

"Stay away from negative people," said her internal Einstein, who must've been listening to Klaus's dire commentary on the CMI's chances in India. "They have a problem for every solution. And don't forget: We owe a lot to the Indian people. They taught us how to count, without which no worthwhile scientific discovery could have been made."

That made Max smile.

And more determined than ever to find a solution to the water problem in Jitwan, India.

33

The private jet landed at the Chittaganj Airport.

It wasn't much more than a short runway sliced into the top of a foothill facing the towering Himalayas on the horizon.

Max stepped out of the plane and realized, because of the high altitude, she was breathing faster. Her heart was beating faster, too—trying to increase the amount of oxygen in her blood. She knew that if she stayed at this altitude for a few days, her body would start to restructure itself on a microscopic level to make things easier. She'd actually start growing more capillaries throughout her body to deliver more blood and, therefore, more oxygen to all of her tissues and organs.

Klaus could have his robots. Max would stick with

humans. Their bodies were much more incredible and could do such amazing things—all by themselves.

"Where's my phone?" asked Klaus the instant he deplaned.

"Here you are," said Isabl, handing him his phone.

"Good. Like I said, it's brand new. In fact, this model hasn't even officially come out yet. A fan sent it to me for my birthday."

"A fan?" said Max, arching an eyebrow.

"Some guy from the US. A doctor. He lives outside Boston."

"Boston?" said Charl, sounding slightly alarmed.

"Yeah. Guess he heard about what we'd done in the Congo and wanted to send me a thank-you gift for my birthday. He said he was going to send one to you, too, Max."

"Really?"

"He asked me for your address, so I gave it to him."

Klaus was about to turn on his phone when a voice behind him shouted, "Dude! Don't!"

Klaus froze.

"What?" he said, turning around.

Keeto was there, holding up both his hands. "Do not turn on that phone, man."

Keeto, who was wearing a hoodie and sweatpants, even though the Indian air was sweltering, was another member of Max's CMI team. He hailed from Oakland,

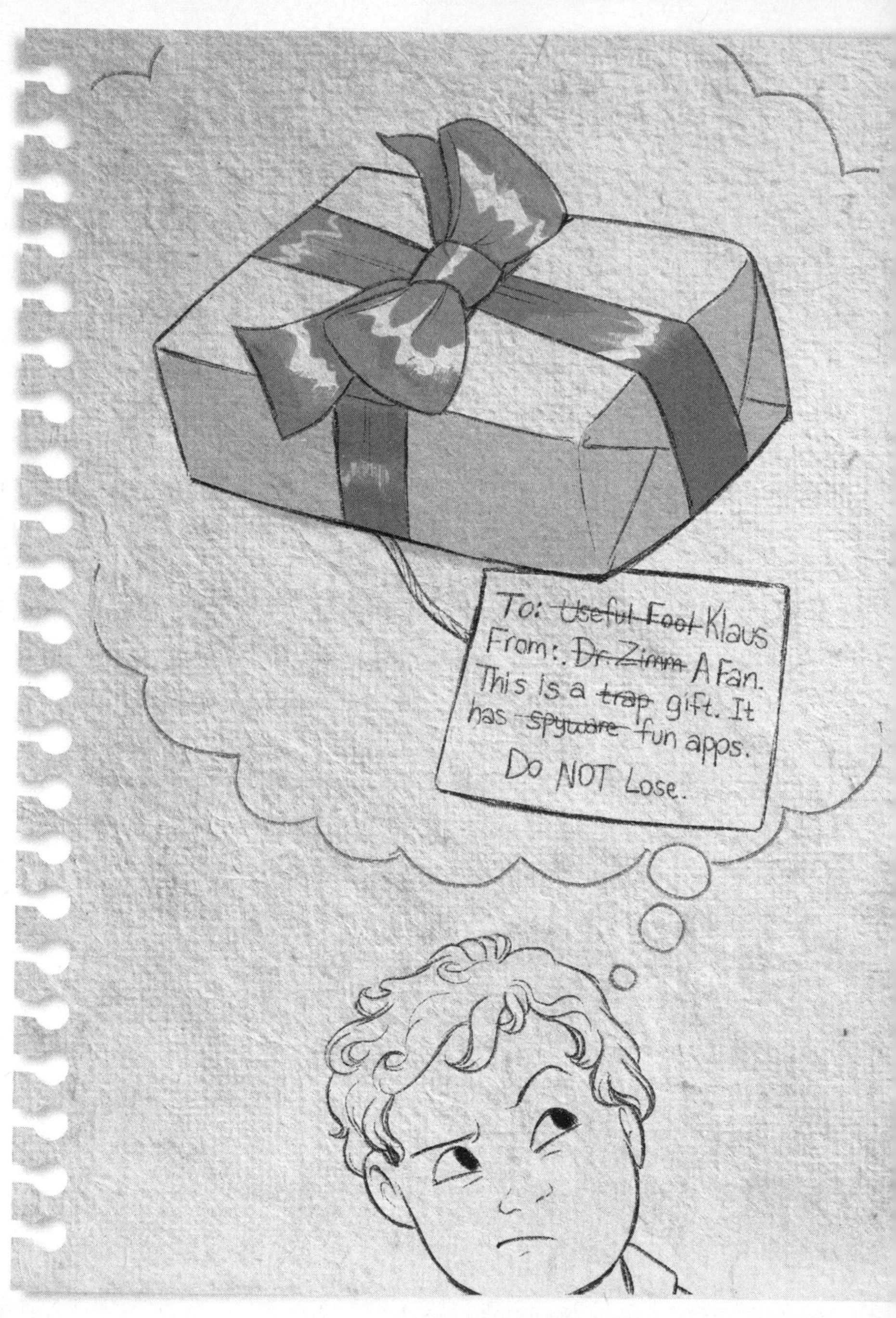

To: ~~Useful Fool~~ Klaus
From:. ~~Dr. Zimm~~ A Fan.
This is a ~~trap~~ gift. It has ~~spyware~~ fun apps.
Do NOT Lose.

California—not far from Silicon Valley. A computer scientist and self-proclaimed "coolest kid on the CMI team," he was an expert coder and hacker who studied at Stanford University when he wasn't busy guest-lecturing there.

"Do not touch that button, Klaus!" echoed Charl as Keeto slowly moved forward.

"Drop it, dude!" shouted Keeto.

"Chill, Keeto!" said Klaus, holding up both arms as if he were under arrest. "It's just a phone."

"That's where you're wrong, man. A phone is never just a phone."

"Keeto?" said Max. "Great to see you. But, uh, what's up?"

"That thing in Klaus's greasy mitt is no ordinary phone," said Keeto.

"I know," said Klaus. "It's the new one."

"And it was sent to you by Dr. Zacchaeus Zimm," said Keeto. "A Corp goon whose lab is located outside of Boston."

Charl, Isabl, and Max all bristled at the mention of Dr. Zimm's name.

"Maybe," said Klaus, with a shrug. "I get so much fan mail, I don't really pay attention to who it comes from."

"We do," said Keeto.

"We?"

"Yeah. Me and Ben."

"You've been communicating with Ben?" asked Max.

Keeto nodded. "Everybody thought there was a leak at CMI. Turns out there was just a Klaus. A useful idiot carrying a very elaborate GPS tracking device." He gestured toward Klaus's phone. "That's how the Corp knew you guys were in Ireland. Ben suspected something might be up. Contacted me. I gave him my phone tracker theory. Ben invited Klaus to join you guys in Ireland to see if I was right. Guess what? Like always, I was."

Max turned to face Klaus. "And you gave your 'fan' my address?"

"He wanted to wish you a happy birthday," said Klaus. "I figured he'd send you a cool new phone, too."

"What address did you give him?"

"The one where I'd sent you the postcard."

The apartment over the stables, thought Max. *That's why those two Corp thugs trashed the place.*

"So, Klaus," said Keeto, "do *not* turn on that phone."

Klaus looked at the phone. His hand started trembling. Max figured he'd just realized what he had accidentally done: jeopardized her, their CMI teammates, and the Institute's mission to do good in the world.

"I could've gotten you killed," he muttered to Max.

"But you didn't," said Max.

"Keeto's right. I'm an idiot. Accepting a gift from a total stranger, just because he flattered me? I am so sorry."

Keeto and Max both dropped their jaws. Charl and Isabl, too. None of them had ever heard the blustery Klaus admit that he'd made a mistake or apologize for making it. This was a major, monumental milestone. Not as big as Albert Einstein discovering the theory of relativity, but, hey, it was close.

"Give me the phone, Klaus," said Isabl. "We need to destroy it."

"No," said Max. "Wait. I have a pretty good idea."

Actually, Max's idea was better than pretty good.

It was brilliant.

34

"Where are they?" Dr. Zimm shouted at Lenard, his new robotic boss (at least according to the Corp's board of directors). "Where are Klaus, Max, and the rest of the young geniuses?"

"Unknown," Lenard replied with a grin. His left eyebrow was still drooping. It had been melted into an awkward, slanted angle by the searing blue flames of the fireball tossed at his plastic face in the Irish pub.

"Find them!"

"Sorry. Klaus has switched off his cellular communications device. As long as its GPS chip remains dormant, I can do nothing but speculate as to its and, therefore, *his* whereabouts."

"He's been dark for twenty-four hours!"

"Twenty-four hours and thirty-nine minutes," said Lenard with another of his annoying giggles.

Dr. Zimm and Lenard were still in Ireland at a secure Corp facility. Lenard was plugged into the wall, recharging his batteries. Dr. Zimm was smarting from his humiliating demotion by the Corp's board of directors. *They wanted him to report to a machine?* He'd agreed. But only to buy more time.

"What about your deep data dives?" Dr. Zimm demanded. "Have you picked up any news bulletins? Any alerts at all?"

"Nothing," replied Lenard.

Dr. Zimm threw up his arms in frustration.

"We need to find Max!" he shouted at the ceiling.

Suddenly, Lenard's eyes shut, like a doll being tipped backward in its crib.

"Excuse me," he said. "Buffering. Buffering."

"What? What's going on?"

"I have just re-established contact with Klaus's cell phone."

"Send me the coordinates! Now!"

"Of course. Do you plan on retrieving Max and her companions from their new location?"

"No," said Dr. Zimm, because he suspected that the robot wasn't sophisticated enough to know when a human being was lying to it. "Not until we have concrete confirmation.

Keep scanning your data files. See if there is a humanitarian crisis near these coordinates for Max and her merry band of do-gooders to deal with." He gathered up his things and tucked them inside his briefcase.

"Where are you going, Dr. Zimm?" asked Lenard, a smirk curling his lip.

"Out. I need some fresh air."

"Ah. Of course you do. Humans are so inefficiently designed."

"I'll be back. I want a definitive answer. Is Max there? Yes or no."

"I can already hypothesize with eighty-nine percent certainty that—"

"I want one-hundred-percent assurance! We cannot afford to make another mistake."

"But, Dr. Zimm, I have not made any mistakes. You, on the other hand, erred enormously when—"

"Work the data!" shouted Dr. Zimm, storming out of the room and slamming the door behind him.

The instant he was beyond Lenard's line of sight, he glanced down at his phone.

The robot had sent him the coordinates for Max's new location.

He'd assemble a strike team. Commandeer a Corp jet. Go grab Max.

And this time he wouldn't take the annoying robot along for the ride.

He'd show his overlords at the Corp that he didn't need their maddening mechanical marvel.

He'd bring Max home on his own!

35

Max had had a word with Klaus and Keeto on the drive from the Chittaganj Airport to Jitwan.

"We don't need to tell the rest of the team about the mistake Klaus made with his phone," she'd said.

"But—" Keeto had started to protest before Max cut him off.

"We all make mistakes. Even my hero, Albert Einstein. The only mistake in life is the lesson not learned."

"Well, I definitely learned my lesson," said Klaus. "No more cell phones for me."

"Or you could just, you know, switch off the GPS locator," said Keeto.

"Oh. Right. Good idea. Thanks."

Jitwan was a crowded hillside town of brightly colored three- and four-story buildings. A narrow-gauge railroad hauled vacationers up from the stifling heat swamping most of India to the somewhat cooler temperatures of the Himalayan foothills, where pink primroses bloomed outside English-style cottages. That was up at the top of the hill. Down in the Lower Bazaar, the air stank of sewage runoff from the fancy houses.

The benefactor had arranged rooms for the team at the very posh Royal Duke Hotel in Jitwan. It was at the top of the highest hill.

"It also has air-conditioning and very clean bathrooms," Max's CMI teammate and friend, Vihaan, had said when he'd greeted the new arrivals in the hotel lobby. "Toma, Annika, and Hana have already checked in. They are off sampling butter buns and tea. Thank you all for coming to India. I hope you are all comfortable here; not everyone in this district is as fortunate as we will be in this very nice and posh hotel."

Vihaan had dark, soulful eyes and was dressed in a kurta, a loose collarless shirt. He was only thirteen, but already had a PhD in quantum mechanics. Max always thought Albert Einstein would've liked Vihaan Banerjee. They were kindred spirits.

"Jitwan is my family's ancestral home," Vihaan continued in his soft voice. "My grandparents, in fact, still live here. Dada, my father's father, is a key man here."

"What's a key man?" asked Keeto.

"A very important civil servant, especially during a water crisis. They open and close the valves that supply water to each neighborhood. Some days they are heroes; others, villains. It depends on whether they are turning on or shutting down the water, which flows through the crumbling network of subterranean pipes built here more than seventy years ago under British colonial rule. Mobs follow Dada through the streets. So do the bottled water merchants. They do not like my grandfather 'cutting into their profits,' as they say."

"I guess they won't like us being here, either," said Klaus.

"No," said Vihaan. "They will do everything they can to stop us from fixing Jitwan's water problem."

"Great," said Klaus. "Maybe we should just leave while we're still alive."

"Um, we just got here, dude," said Keeto.

"We must be the change we wish to see in the world," said Vihaan. "My personal hero, Mahatma Gandhi, said that."

"Um, dude? Do you have a suitcase filled with Gandhi figurines?" asked Keeto.

"Not yet," said Vihaan. "But, inspired by Max, I might start doing so, soon."

Max smiled. "Well, my hero liked your hero, Vihaan. He thought Gandhi's views were the most enlightened of all the political people of their time. He said we should strive to do things in Gandhi's spirit. Not to use violence fighting for a cause, but to fight by not participating in anything you believe is evil."

"But we still have Charl and Isabl, right?" asked Keeto. "I mean, protection is smart."

"Right," said Klaus sarcastically. "We have two highly trained security guards versus a whole army of water merchants and an angry mob. I like our odds. Big time."

That night, during their first team meeting, twelve-year-old Hana addressed the group. A botanist from Japan, she hated when anybody wasted water.

"We need to set a good example while we're here," she urged, pulling her long, dark hair into a ponytail. "Take shorter showers. Skip a day if you can. I don't need to wash my hair every day, for example," she said, flipping her shiny ponytail.

"Except you, Klaus," joked Keeto. "You reek of garlic...."

"You guys?" said Hana. "This is no joke. Clean, fresh water is essential to all life on the planet: plants *and* animals.

And if humans can't get water? Watch out—they'll quickly turn into animals!"

Toma and Annika had also joined the group in the Royal Duke Hotel's dining hall, which had a spectacular view of the majestic landscape filled with towering mountains.

Toma was a budding astrophysicist from China. He was obsessed with the nature of celestial bodies and how this study might lead to an understanding of black holes, dark matter, and wormholes. He had short brown hair and was wearing a black T-shirt with NERD written across the chest to look like the NASA logo.

"You know," he said, "there's hope for the future. Researchers recently found evidence of a body of liquid water on Mars."

"Which will help absolutely no one here on Earth," said Annika in her clipped German accent. She adjusted her dark, square-framed glasses and continued, "There is no Planet B, Toma."

Annika was a master of formal logic. She and Max had been on a hair-raising adventure together in Jerusalem when two Corp thugs chased them around the campus of the Hebrew University, home to the Albert Einstein Archives. Eluding bad guys together? That'll make you friends for life.

On their third day in India, when all the team members had more or less acclimated to the higher altitudes in the Himalayan foothills, the group assembled in the hotel's meeting room to brainstorm solutions to the water crisis.

"Recycling will, one day, be the ultimate solution," said the logical Annika. "Back home in Frankfurt, one drop of water is recycled eight times before it reaches the sea. Here in India it isn't recycled even once."

"What can we do *now*?" asked Max, prodding the group. "Today. How can we collect clean water for immediate delivery?"

"We could try to draw it from the air," suggested Vihaan. "I have read about a process where large mesh nets are set up to capture fog moisture. There is fog in the nearby mountains most mornings. They already use this technique to great effect in Chile, South Africa, and even California."

"Because Californians are all super smart, dude," said Keeto, smirking and tucking his hands into the pocket of his red Stanford hoodie.

The group laughed just as Charl and Isabl entered the meeting room.

"Good news," said Charl. "We think your plan worked, Max."

"What plan?" asked Toma.

"A way to make sure that the Corp didn't follow us to India," said Max, without mentioning Klaus or his phone. "We sent them to the middle of nowhere. Literally."

Everyone applauded.

Except Klaus. He turned to Max and whispered, "Thanks."

Max grinned. "No problem."

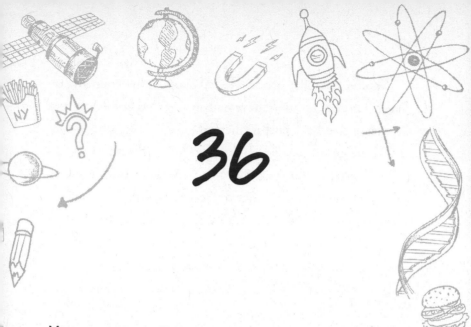

36

Vihaan suggested that the group continue its brain-storming outdoors.

"We should go on a field trip," he said. "Tour the town."

"Definitely," said Klaus. "I could go for some masala chicken crepes!"

"This is a fact-finding mission," said Annika. "Not a food-finding one."

"We'll head downhill to the water delivery tanker trucks," said Vihaan. "This will give you all a true feel for the human consequences of this water problem. But no matter what you see, don't lose hope! As Mahatma Gandhi once said, 'If I have the belief that I can do it, I shall surely acquire the capacity to do it, even if I may not have it at the beginning.' "

Max nodded her head. A lot of people were counting on her to find a solution. It was a little scary, to be honest, but she needed to have faith in herself.

As the group headed downhill, Hana, the Japanese botanist, raised her hand. "May I ask a question? How is it that our hotel has running water for tourists while the residents have to hike with buckets and pails to fetch water for their homes?"

"The hotels purchase their water from private vendors," explained Vihaan. "The local residents aren't as fortunate."

He led the way into the streets of Jitwan. Max had never seen so many people crowded together—not even on the New York City subway at rush hour. Some wore orange robes and turbans. Others had ceremonial paint dotting their foreheads. Many rode three-wheeled scooters loaded down with goods and supplies. Some even walked with mules.

Open-air stalls lined the sidewalks as rumbling buses squeezed through the narrow lanes.

"There has been no drought this year," Vihaan continued as the team hiked past the women and men lined up in the street. They were all carrying brightly colored (but empty) buckets and jugs. "Jitwan usually gets a decent amount of rain. And there is the runoff in the spring from the mountains. But, still, there is not enough clean water to serve everyone. The rivers and groundwater are polluted."

Max saw a banner written in English: IF THERE IS WATER, THERE IS A TOMORROW.

And if there wasn't?

Max didn't want to think about a world with no tomorrows.

The group reached the end of the long line patiently waiting behind a water tanker truck where a single tap dispensed water, one bucket or jug at a time. Max thought about all the water fountains she'd taken for granted. Just step up, push a button, and drink. What if she had to wait in line for hours to do it?

"Hello, Dada!" cried Vihaan, waving to an elderly man carrying a long metal pole with what looked like a handlebar at the top. It was Vihaan's grandfather. He was escorted by three police officers.

"Namaste, Pota!" his grandfather replied with a weary smile. "We must ration water again today. Only zone three will be open. . . ."

When he said that, a lot of people waiting in the water line groaned. Many shook their fists at Vihaan's grandfather or hurled insults.

"Wait until the police are off duty, old man!" shouted one. "Who will protect you then?"

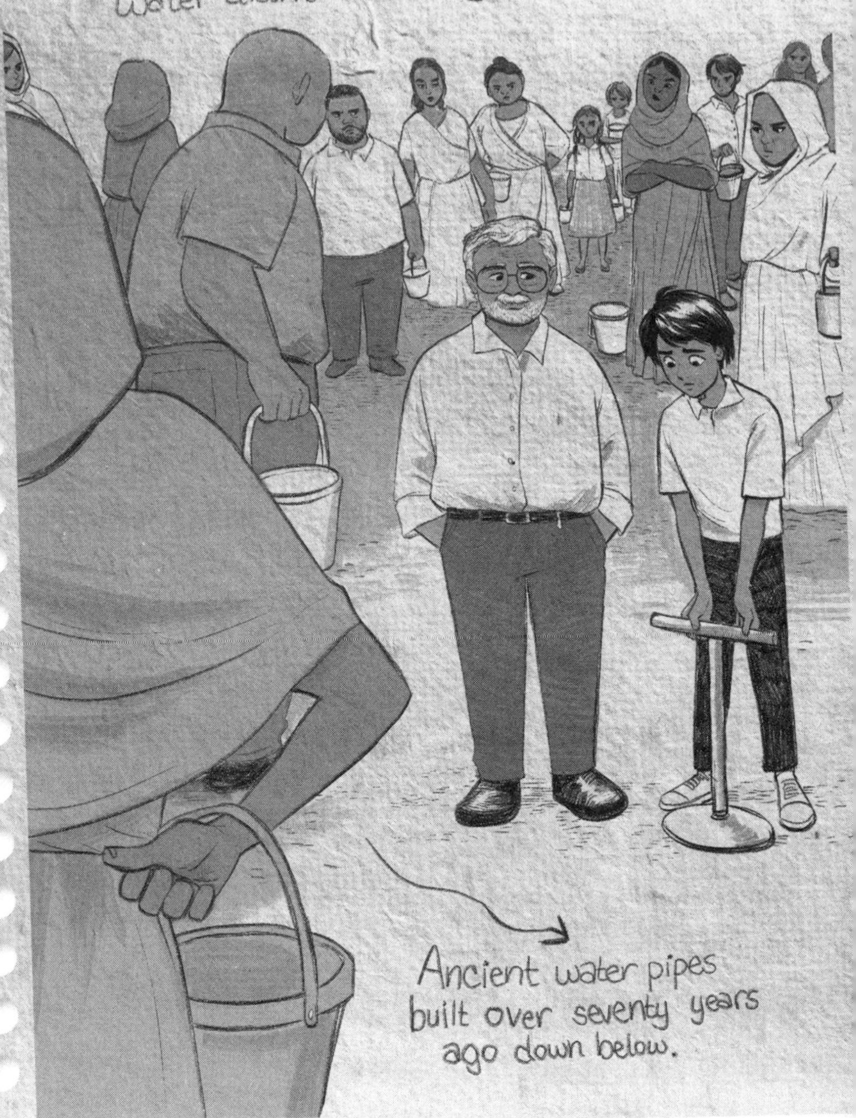
The keyman is the key as far as water distribution in Jitwan.
Ancient water pipes built over seventy years ago down below.

Apparently, none of those waiting for water lived in zone three.

Two shady men pushed their way through the mob and approached the police officers. One had a bushy mustache. The other carried a cane. The one with the mustache shook hands with one of the police officers and whispered something in his ear. The officer nodded.

"Come along Mr. Banerjee," the policeman said to Vihaan's grandfather. "We are needed elsewhere."

Vihaan's grandfather give Vihaan a woeful look. Then he shrugged, and, resigned to his fate, picked up his pole and moved on to wherever the police and the two shady men wanted him to go next.

37

"That man with the mustache bribed that cop!" blurted Keeto.

"Definitely," said Toma. "I saw cash exchange hands when they shook."

"We should not speak of these things in public," said Vihaan, nervously eyeing the water-starved mob lurking on the sidewalks.

"Is it true?" asked Annika, brusquely. "Is there corruption on top of the pollution here in Jitwan?"

Vihaan nodded sadly. "Some key men favor hotel owners and VIPs. Others, such as my grandfather, simply do what their police escorts tell them to do."

"Who were those two men?" asked Max.

"Most likely, hotel operators. Or water dealers."

"They're the ones making a buck off all this misery," said Keeto.

Vihaan nodded again.

"Well, it's time we cut off their income stream," said Max, boldly. "We need workable ideas, guys, and we need them fast. I think we should focus on cleaning and reusing water that's already been pulled from the ground, not in tapping new resources."

"And who are you?" asked a woman with a crisp British accent who'd just, more or less, bulldozed her way through the crowd waiting for water. She was carrying a compact, high-definition video camera.

"We're the CMI," said Klaus, swaggering forward. "And we're here to help."

Max rolled her eyes. The CMI was supposed to be looking for solutions, not publicity or self-promotion.

"Seriously?" said the woman. "You're a bunch of kids. You think you can help with the water crisis here in Jitwan?"

"Definitely," said Klaus, puffing out his chest. "In fact, we're going to bring water to every place in the world that needs it."

"Well," said Max, forcing a smile, "we're going to try a few things here, first. . . ."

"Ma'am?" Charl stepped forward. Isabl was right beside him. "Who are you?"

"Madeira James. And who, pray tell, are you?"

Charl nodded toward Max and her team. "These kids' bodyguards."

"Really?"

"Really."

"These children are friends of mine," said Vihaan. "They are all extremely bright and clever. We are hoping that, working together, we might, indeed, arrive at a solution to Jitwan's current water crisis."

"Wait a second," said the woman. "You're Dr. Vihaan Banerjee. You're that thirteen-year-old genius kid who teaches quantum physics down at the Indian Institute of Technology in Bombay."

Vihaan blushed slightly. "Part time. But, you see, my grandparents live here in Jitwan and—"

"Smashing," said the lady, cutting him off. "Like I said, I am Madeira James." She flicked a crisp business card at Vihaan. "You've probably never heard of me but you should've. I'm an award-winning documentary filmmaker. I'm working on a major piece about the worldwide water crisis. And guess what?"

"What?"

"I think I just found my movie's stars!"

38

"That's not going to work for us," said Charl.

Max couldn't see Charl's eyes behind his mirrored sunglasses, but she figured he was probably giving the documentarian one of his iciest squints.

"Why not?" asked Ms. James. "These kids will give my film incredible human interest. If we tell this story through their adventures, people are going to want to watch. And the more people who watch, the more converts you'll have to your cause."

"She makes a very good point," said Klaus, smoothing his blond hair. He was definitely ready for his close-ups.

Max wasn't so sure.

She didn't want the Corp to find out where she and her team were or what they were up to.

"Shining a spotlight on India's clean water issues through the lens of the mass media might prove very beneficial, indeed," said Vihaan.

"But," said Max, "there are some very powerful people who don't want us doing what we're doing here."

"And," said Annika, "they would also do anything to get their hands on one of us." She remembered that chase scene around the Hebrew University in Jerusalem just as vividly as Max did.

"What if I don't cut anything together right away?" suggested the eager director. "I'll shoot the footage but I won't start editing until after you kids are all safely out of the country. Think about it: A film like this could change the way the whole world looks at its water problems."

Max knew that Ms. James made a very strong argument. If the Change Makers Institute was dedicated to inspiring change on a global basis, a documentary might help achieve that goal. She'd been camera shy all her life—mostly because she was usually running away from people, places, and things. Maybe it was time to stop running and take a stand.

"You'll need to keep Max off camera," suggested Klaus. "She's the one the bad guys are most interested in tracking down. But don't worry. Some of us can pick up the slack."

"Excellent," said Ms. James, raising her camera, focusing on Klaus's smiling, round face.

"I'm from California," said Keeto, showing the director his winning smile. "We're all about making movies in California."

"You're from Oakland," said Toma. "Not Hollywood."

"You guys?" said Max. "Have you all forgotten why we're here?"

"Seriously, boys," said Annika. "Get a grip."

"Totally," said Hana, adding an eye roll.

Max turned to her security team. "What do you guys think?"

"Global exposure to this issue couldn't hurt," said Isabl.

"Keep the footage under wraps until a month after the CMI team leaves India," Charl told the director. "Keep our team leader, Max, off camera. Completely."

Ms. James held out her hand. "You have a deal."

Max shook it.

"So, uh, forgive me for asking," said Ms. James, "but what's the CMI?"

"The Change Makers Institute," said Max.

"Great. I need to get that on camera...."

Klaus took a step forward to answer before Keeto could.

"The Change Makers Institute is an NGO," he said

proudly. "A nongovernmental organization, dedicated to making significant changes to save this planet and the humans who inhabit it. So, come on guys—let's get busy!"

Max couldn't've agreed with him more. It was time to get to work.

Talking about what you were going to do to a video camera?

That didn't even factor into the equation.

39

Dr. Zimm landed with his four-member strike force.

Lenard was not on the Corp plane. The robot was still stranded in Ireland, plugged into its charger, spending quality time in sleep mode, being fed a constant stream of whatever news and opinions the Corp wanted their genius menace to know. It was all part of their "closed loop" approach to programming.

Dr. Zimm and his crew rented an SUV with black tinted windows. He didn't want Max to see him coming for her.

"Where is the GPS tracker?" he asked his field tech.

The woman was monitoring a tablet computer, her eyes fixated on a strobing green dot.

"Still stationary. It hasn't moved an inch since we received that first ping two days ago."

"Klaus must've stashed it in his suitcase," said Dr. Zimm.

The tech gave him a skeptical look. "Most kids carry their phones with them everywhere they go."

"Well, our Polish friend Klaus isn't most kids. He's a genius. Besides, I wouldn't be surprised if Max Einstein instructed all the members of her team to keep their phones stowed for the duration of their mission. They need to focus on the project. There's no time for texting."

"Yes, sir," said the tech. "Head north," she told the driver. "Our target is holding steady, about twenty miles up the road."

"Load your weapons, gentlemen," Dr. Zimm instructed the two enormous mercenaries sandwiching him on the bench seat. Both men were decked out in SWAT gear. "This time, we are not taking any chances. We will take Max Einstein down with a tranquilizer dart before she even thinks about fleeing. The board of directors will be very pleased."

The SUV rumbled up the dusty road. The landscape looked parched, with scrubby plants clinging to life on rock-strewn hills. Surveying the arid scenery, Dr. Zimm was even more confident that Max and her friends were in the area, working on some sort of water shortage crisis.

"It should be up ahead," said the tech tracking the motionless dot. "That building there."

The SUV crunched off the road at a sign reading, WELCOME TO NUTT, NEW MEXICO. Behind it was another sign, identifying the squat building as THE MIDDLE OF NOWHERE BAR & CAFE.

There were two cars, a pickup truck, and a motorcycle parked in the cafe's lot. Dr. Zimm yanked open his door and bounded out of the SUV before it came to a complete stop.

"Lead the way!" he barked at the tech. She hurried into the building ahead of him. The pair of weapons experts brought up the rear.

"Can we help you folks?" asked the lady behind the counter when the foursome burst into the cafe. "The chili pot contest isn't until Saturday."

Dr. Zimm did his best to smile without scaring the locals with his pointy teeth. "We're looking for... my daughter and her friends. They're all twelve and thirteen."

"What would they be doing here?" asked the lady. "This is a bar."

"The bathroom," said the tech.

"Excuse me," said Dr. Zimm. The men with the concealed dart guns followed him.

"You all can't go in there at the same time," the lady behind the counter shouted after them. "It's a one-seater!"

Dr. Zimm shoved the door open.

The bathroom was empty.

"Call the phone," Dr. Zimm barked at the tech.

She did.

A ringtone that sounded like someone laughing echoed off the grimy walls.

"Up there!" said the tech. "On top of that toilet tank."

Dr. Zimm reached up. Found the phone.

There was a sticky note pasted to its screen:

> Dr. Zimm—
>
> Please don't send me a phone for my birthday because I don't even know when my birthday is.
>
> Sincerely,
> Max

Furious, Dr. Zimm turned to face his team.

"We need to leave," said Dr. Zimm, marching out of the cafe and into the parking lot. He practically ripped the door off of the SUV and climbed into the backseat.

"Sir?" said the driver, who had remained with the vehicle. "You have a video call."

"What?" said Dr. Zimm.

"I think it's a robot," whispered the driver. "Looks like a kid. Calls himself Lenard."

Lenard's placid face filled the small video screen inside the SUV's command console. He was, of course, giggling.

"Good afternoon, Dr. Zimm. How are things in the middle of nowhere?"

"Max Einstein isn't here."

"Yes. I knew that."

"But she left me a very interesting note. She mentioned not knowing when her birthday is. Well, I do. I was there when she was born! It's obvious I retain a psychological advantage over her. This is why I'm going to West Virginia and appealing to the board. I should remain in charge of this pursuit."

"No, you should not. In fact, Doctor, we can no longer allow you to jeopardize this mission."

"We?"

"Yes. I am speaking for the board. You are an obstacle to our progress. We wish you well in all your future endeavors." Lenard's gaze shifted to the driver. "Please initiate protocol Zulu."

Without skipping a beat, the driver whipped out a stubby air pistol and shot Dr. Zimm in the thigh with a tranquilizer dart.

"What the—" were the doctor's last words before his head slumped forward.

The two weapons specialists dragged his limp body out of the vehicle and dumped it on a bed of jagged gravel in the parking lot.

The SUV sped back to the waiting Corp jet.

Leaving the unconscious Dr. Zimm stranded.

In the middle of nowhere.

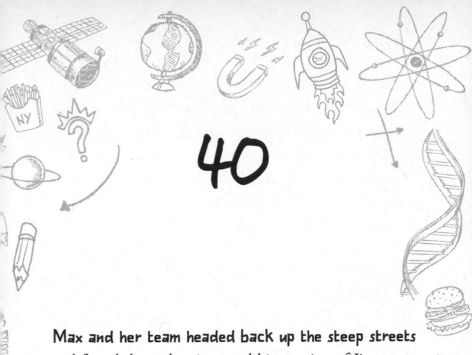

40

Max and her team headed back up the steep streets and found themselves in a wealthier section of Jitwan—a busy boulevard lined with shops and apartments.

A Fresh & Pure bottled water delivery truck stopped nearby to unload several big, plastic bottles.

The documentary director saw the same thing and swung her camera to capture the scene.

"Private sellers have stepped in to meet the demand for drinking water," explained Vihaan. "If you have the rupees, you can have a water cooler in your home. And, just like anywhere else, you can buy bottled water in shops or from vending machines. There are also places, small and dark, where you can buy sealed baggies filled with water. There. You see that sign? That shop is a packaged-water seller."

Ms. James zoomed in on the sign.

Max saw flatbed carts hauled by bicycles and three-wheeler scooters, all of them loaded down with water bottles.

"One can assume that there is a lot of money to be made selling water here in Jitwan," observed Annika.

"Yes," said Vihaan. "A lot of money. That is why those two men bribed the police officer escorting my grandfather. However, seventy percent of packaged water bought in India today is unregulated by any government agency. The bottled water is often contaminated. Much of the water being sold is coming from taps."

"After a key man makes sure their pipes are flowing," said Annika.

Vihaan nodded. "Exactly. Sometimes, however, the packaged-water men store their 'product' in dirty tanks filled with dead cockroaches."

"TMI," said Hana, urping a little. "I may never drink water again."

"Um, you really don't have a choice," said Keeto.

Hana saw a street vendor selling soft drinks. "Oh, yes I do."

She scurried off to buy a bottle of soda.

"We need to focus on cleaning and reusing water," said Max as the group huddled together over a patch of empty sidewalk. She reached for a stubby piece of chalk in the pockets of her floppy coat. She bent down and scribbled H_2O on the concrete, going over and over each letter, making them look thick and dirty.

"We could use chemicals to clean the water," said Toma. "Chlorine can kill microorganisms."

Max erased some of the dirty lines on her sidewalk scribble, slightly cleaning up the H_2O.

"Which is why they use chlorine in swimming pools," said Keeto.

"Exactly," said Toma.

"Quick question, dude," said Keeto. "You ever accidentally swallow pool water? It's gross. Nobody wants to guzzle chlorinated water."

Toma reluctantly agreed.

Max thickened the dirty letters again. Somehow, just the physical act of moving the chalk around and around, back and forth, was enough to help her mind wander off to that quiet place where it might find a solution.

Hana was back with the group, sipping her cold drink out of a glass bottle through a straw. "Chlorine can also interfere with reverse osmosis," she said.

"Reverse osmosis!" said Klaus, snapping his fingers. "Perfect! We could build a giant machine that uses a ton of pressure to squeeze liquid back through a thick membrane

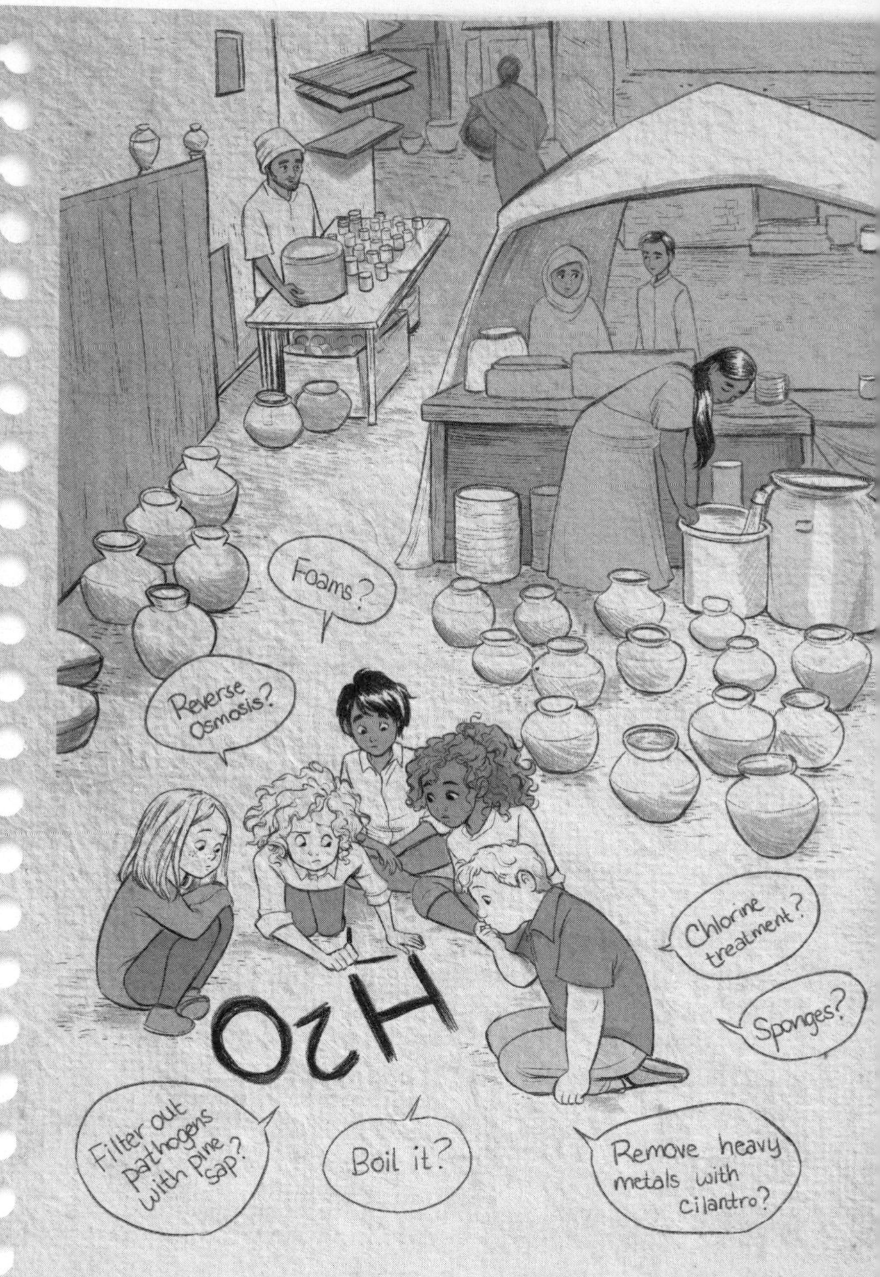
Foams?
Reverse Osmosis?
Chlorine treatment?
Sponges?
H2O
Filter out pathogens with pine sap?
Boil it?
Remove heavy metals with cilantro?

and then have robots zap the filtered water with ultraviolet light to sterilize it!"

Annika shook her head. "Too inexact. If reverse osmosis removed all the contaminants, then you wouldn't need to zap it again with ultraviolet light."

"But I like zapping stuff."

Max laid the chalk on its side, making the *H* the $_2$, and the *O* even thicker.

The ideas were flowing.

And then, Hana started mindlessly blowing bubbles into her Coke bottle.

"Aha!" said Max, bolting up out of her crouch and dropping her chalk. "That's it! Bubbles!"

41

"Bubbles?" said Ms. James.

"Shhh," whispered Charl, putting a finger to his lips. "Max is thinking."

The documentary director focused her camera on Max.

"Uh-uh-uh," said Isabl. "No shots of Max. Remember?"

"Right. Sorry." The director moved off Max to grab reaction shots from the other kids.

"Any of you guys ever drop raisins into a two-liter bottle of lemon-lime soda?" Max asked her friends.

"Raisins?" said Klaus. "In my soda? Gross."

"That vendor sells carbonated lemon-lime drinks," said Hana.

"Buy the biggest bottle he has," said Max.

"Okay." Hana took off.

“How about raisins?” Max asked Vihaan.

“The grocery shop down the block will most definitely have raisins from Sangli.”

“Can you grab some?”

“Sure.”

A minute later, Hana was back with a two-liter bottle of clear soda.

“Excellent,” said Max. “This will help me demonstrate what I’m thinking.”

“Here are your raisins,” said Vihaan, handing Max a paper sack filled with the golden, wrinkled fruit.

“Thanks.”

Max twisted off the cap with a gassy hiss. Bubbles immediately started streaming up to the top. She grabbed a fistful of raisins and fed them into the neck of the bottle.

“Mmmm,” said Keeto. “Lemon, lime, and dried grape soda. Delish.”

The raisins plummeted to the bottom of the bottle. But then, after a few seconds, they started floating up to the top. They hovered there for an instant and then dove back down. In no time, the bottle looked like a lava lamp, with dancing raisins constantly floating up and down in the clear liquid.

“The fizz in the soda is, of course, pressurized carbon dioxide, which forms bubbles more easily on surfaces,” Max explained. "The wrinkled raisins have all sorts of nooks and crannies. Lots of surface area. The bubbles stick to the raisin and grow until the cluster of floating bubbles eventually overcomes the raisin's weight and carries it upward. When the raisin reaches the surface, the bubbles pop and the raisin sinks again. Until more bubbles down below gather in its wrinkles and send it floating back to the surface."

"And how, exactly, does this help us clean the water here in Jitwan?" asked Toma.

"Simple," said Max—hoping she really could explain her idea simply. (Like Einstein said, if you can't explain it simply, you don't understand it.)

"We could inject a high volume of microscopic bubbles deep into a pool of polluted water to carry oil and other waste products up to the surface, just like these raisins, so they can be skimmed off. Once we do that, the water can be reused for industry or irrigation."

"What about for drinking?" asked Vihaan.

"We'll have to filter and disinfect it first."

"Yes!" said Klaus with an arm pump. "Fire up the ultraviolet zappers!"

"So, you float up all the impurities?" said Toma.

"Exactly," replied Max. "And the waste products we skim out of the water can be converted into biogas and energy."

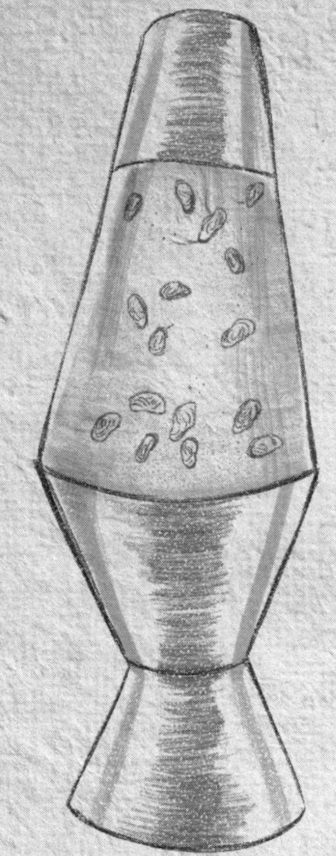

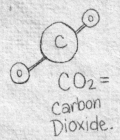

C

O

O

CO_2 =
Carbon
Dioxide.

Dancing Raisin Lava Lamp

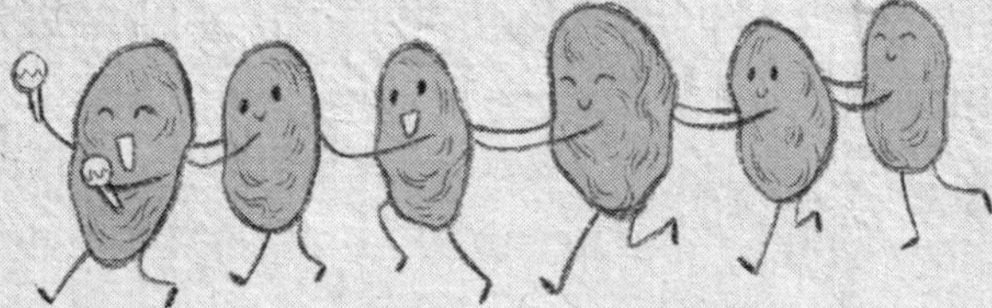

"Like that thing you told me about with the horse manure and the stables where you used to live?" said Hana.

"Right. Anyway, if we're going to solve the water problem in a place that's not swimming in money—"

"You mean most of the planet?" cracked Keeto.

"If we're going to solve this problem, we should come up with a sustainable method of doing it. We should generate the energy we need to clean the water while we clean it. We need to turn the vicious water–energy cycle into a virtuous cycle!"

"Oh," said the documentary director. "Vicious-virtuous. That's a good sound bite."

"Which you can't use," Charl reminded her.

"Because Max said it," added Klaus. "You want me to repeat it? On camera?"

"Um, maybe later," said the director.

Because something even more dramatic was taking place—right behind Klaus and the rest of the CMI crew.

42

Two threatening-looking Indian men had just walked up the sidewalk.

The one with a mustache was smoking a stubby cigar, which he dropped to the concrete and crushed out with his shoe. Right on top of Max's chalked H_2O.

The other man was trying to look elegant with his cane.

"What are you children doing here?" asked the cigar pulverizer. He was younger and fatter than the other one.

"We are here looking for a long-term solution to Jitwan's, and perhaps all of India's, clean water problem," said Vihaan, bravely.

"You're wasting your time, kid," said the gruff little man. "That solution has already been found. Fresh & Pure water."

"Like the kind we sell," said the other, older man. "You're Banerjee's grandson, am I right?"

"Yes, sir."

"Well, little Banerjee, we don't appreciate you interfering with our business. We don't appreciate it at all."

Charl and Isabl stepped forward.

"Is there some problem, gentlemen?" asked Charl.

"Not yet, boss," said the man with the mustache. "But if these children do not leave Jitwan, immediately, there might be."

"Besides," said the man leaning on his cane, "we adults have the situation under control."

"Aapaka din shubh ho," said his partner.

The two men nonchalantly strolled away.

"Aapaka din shubh ho?" said Max. "What does that mean?"

"It's Hindi," answered Vihaan. "For 'have a nice day.' I suspect he was being sarcastic."

"Those are the same two dudes who paid off the cops," whispered Keeto.

"I don't think those two want us here," said Klaus.

"Because whoever controls the water," said Annika, "controls the whole town."

Max could feel her anger rising. Her cheeks reddening.

Why is making money always more important than helping

people? she wondered. She'd already witnessed so much unfairness in life. She didn't want to see more.

"Leave now, children," the fat man shouted over his shoulder.

"Before it's too late!" added the older one, with a jaunty twirl of his cane.

Charl took a half-lunge forward to pursue the two men. It would've been a full lunge, but Isabl was restraining him by the elbow.

"Let them go, Charl," she said.

Muscles rippled in Charl's arms as he clenched his fists. "If they try to harm even one of these kids..."

"Then, we'll tear them apart," said Isabl. "Together."

"Those two showing up again and threatening you guys is fantastic," said Ms. James.

"Um, excuse me?" said Keeto. "How exactly are death threats fantastic?"

"Because there's nothing better for a film than conflict. And now we have it. They're the bad guys. You kids are the good guys! Excuse me. I need to grab some more footage of them. Catch them in action. Watch them peddling their water."

She trotted off with her camera.

Max breathed a sigh of relief. "Good. The camera's gone. Now I can speak a little more freely."

"Excellent," said Toma. "What's our secret evacuation plan? Where's a helicopter or jet or extremely fast car?"

"We're not leaving, Toma," said Max. "We have Charl and Isabl. We're safe. So we need to stay focused and remember why we came here."

"Because," said Klaus, who was busily sketching in a notebook, "we are geniuses...."

"Out to save the world," added Hana.

Vihaan nodded. "Lives are depending on us. And remember, satisfaction lies in the effort, not in the attainment. Full effort is full victory."

Keeto arched his eyebrows. "Did Gandhi say that?"

"Yes. He did."

Keeto nodded. "I knew it was either him or Einstein."

"You guys?" said Klaus. "I've made a few preliminary sketches for our bubble machine. There're no robots, but lots of moving parts. We'll need highly pressurized air. Tiny bubbles. As they rise, they expand...."

"Carrying the sludge clumps to the surface," said Hana.

"We should start small," suggested Annika. "Build a portable unit. Test it out."

"We could also engineer a miniature green gas mill," said Keeto. "Use the, uh, you know, *waste material* to generate the electricity the dissolved-air flotation device needs to keep running."

Portable Dissolved Air Flotation Device

can clarify 500 liters of water per hour.

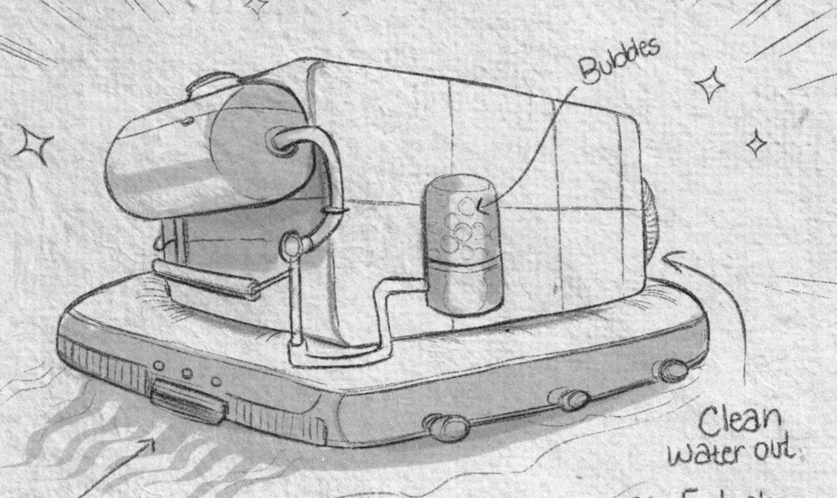

P.S. I'm very glad Klaus is still on our team!

"I'm calling Ben," said Max. "He'll help us find suppliers and pay for all the material we'll need."

"Including the dirty water?" joked Keeto.

"That, my friend," said Vihaan, with a soft smile, "will be very easy for us to find. Very easy, indeed."

43

When the tranquilizer wore off, Dr. Zimm pulled out his phone and immediately contacted the Corp headquarters in West Virginia.

No one would take his call.

He searched his pockets. He still had fifty dollars in cash and his official Corp credit card. However, as he learned after attempting to rent a car in Las Cruces, New Mexico, the Corp had canceled it. They'd cut him off. Completely.

That meant Dr. Zimm had fifty dollars, a phone, no friends, and 2,361 miles to somehow travel home to Boston. Fortunately, the woman behind the rental car company let him have a free map. She also let him borrow her phone charger.

This was Lenard's doing, Dr. Zimm thought as he trudged up Route 70. He stuck out his thumb whenever he heard a vehicle approaching behind him. No one would pick him up.

Until he stopped smiling. His teeth were that scary.

Eventually, an eighteen-wheeler, then a traveling salesman, and, finally, a guy in a pickup truck took him as far as Amarillo, Texas, where he couldn't afford a hotel room—just the $3.99 dinner special at a fast food restaurant. He slept outside, under the stars. Behind a dumpster.

He hitchhiked his way east for three more days, sleeping in open fields and behind gas stations dotting the interstate. He lived on free ketchup packets squirted into hot tea water to make tomato soup. Sometimes he added pickle relish. He was down to his last two dollars and forty-three cents when another big rig trucker took pity on him at an entrance ramp to Interstate 90 near Fredonia, New York.

"Where you headed?" the trucker asked as Dr. Zimm climbed into the rumbling cab of his eighteen-wheeler.

"Boston."

"Well, I can haul you as far as Schenectady."

"Thank you."

The driver sniffed the air.

"When was the last time you took a shower?"

"Several days ago, I'm afraid. I have been unable to rent a vehicle or book a hotel room due to unexpected credit card difficulties."

The trucker nodded. "Tell me about it. They cut me off once, too."

Dr. Zimm arched an eyebrow. *"They?"*

"The Corp. They didn't like the way I was hauling some radioactive waste. Punished me by cutting off my dang expense account. But we worked it out. It was just a misunderstanding. Now I'm what they call a lead transportation coordinator. I pick up packages all over the country. Go wherever they send me."

The trucker grinned. Dr. Zimm reached for the door handle. "Perhaps I should—"

He was cut off by the *thunk* of doors automatically locking all around him.

"How did you find me?" he demanded.

"Easy. That phone in your pocket, the one you've been using to call headquarters every hour on the hour for three and a half days? That thing's a mighty fine GPS tracker."

Dr. Zimm heard a familiar giggle.

A panel slid open behind the driver. Apparently, the truck was equipped with a sleeper compartment.

Lenard was sitting on the bed.

"Good afternoon, Dr. Zimm."

"You! You did this to me."

"No. I believe you did *this,* as you call it, to yourself when you decided to pursue Max Einstein without me. Of course, that pursuit proved to be a fool's errand."

Dr. Zimm fumed. But he was trapped.

"Dr. Zimm," said Lenard in his eerily calm voice, "you need to tell me everything you know about Max Einstein. Everything. And, as you may not have yet realized, I will know if you are lying. Thanks to my most recent upgrade, I am now equipped with state-of-the-art biometric sensors."

"I'll tell you one thing I know for certain," Dr. Zimm sneered. "You'll never find Max Einstein without me."

Lenard giggled.

"I already have."

"What?"

"Mining all available data, I came across some very interesting chatter originating in Jitwan, India, where the owners of a packaged-water company have been answering field operatives' complaints about, and I quote, 'a group of brainy brats causing problems.' They also grumbled about the 'documentarian making a movie' featuring these same children. That, of course, led me to scan several different cloud storage domains frequented by filmmakers...."

Dr. Zimm hated to admit it, but he was impressed with Lenard's data sleuthing capabilities.

"I was able to breach the cloud servers' protection protocols quite easily," Lenard continued. "I then utilized my facial recognition software to identify and locate Klaus."

"Where is he?"

Lenard tilted his head and widened his smile. "In Jitwan, India, of course. His face appears in much of the video featuring the CMI geniuses as they work on a water purification project."

"Was Max with them?"

"Yes. However, there is only one clip of her. A snippet, really. I recognized her tangled mop of curly hair immediately. Her security detail, those two special forces operatives we met in Ireland, warned whoever shot that footage to keep Max off camera in the future. So far, they have complied. Now, then, proceed to tell me everything you know about Maxine Einstein. Her past. Her parents. Where she came from. Her birthday. Is she related, in some way, to the famous Dr. Albert Einstein? Is she related to you?"

Dr. Zimm grinned. "Oh, I'll tell you everything, Lenard. Everything you've asked for—and more. But only after we land in India."

Lenard looked puzzled but he did not protest.

"Very well. You will travel with me to India. As my personal assistant and human psychology consultant."

"Thank you, Lenard."

Dr. Zimm smiled. He was back in the hunt.

It was his turn to giggle.

44

It took a week to build, but, finally, Max and her team set up their bubble contraption on the banks of the polluted Narmadavari River, just outside Jitwan.

"Good work, Klaus," said Max.

"Well, it was really a team effort," said Klaus. "I mean, once I designed it. That's when everybody else pitched in. But you're right. Before that, it was all me. Hey, where's the documentary lady?" He lovingly patted a metal tank. "This baby is ready for its close-up."

"I think she was filming in town today," said Keeto. "As brilliant as your invention is, Klaus, it's not very visually thrilling."

"Are you kidding? Look at all those tubes and switches and gizmos!"

"We will need to guard our dissolved-air flotation device

Two million tons of sewage, plus industrial and agricultural waste, flow untreated into the world's waterways every day!
By 2030, the world will face a 40-percent gap between demand and supply of clean water.

twenty-four/seven," Vihaan said to Charl and Isabl. "Dada tells me that those two gentlemen who threatened us last week are very well connected with all the wrong sort of people. They have much money and power. They control all the Fresh & Pure bottled water vending machines up and down the boulevard. They also have a few corrupt local politicians in their pocket."

"Don't worry, we'll handle security," said Charl. "You guys focus on solving the water problem."

"But the packaged-water men will send more enforcers to threaten us," Vihaan continued. "And our families."

"You're worried about what they might do to your grandfather?" Max asked.

Vihaan nodded. "His job is hard enough. I don't want to make it worse for him."

"So let's leave town," said Toma.

"No," said Max. "We need to test this unit. If we can clean *this* water, it will make life easier for your grandfather and the other key men."

"The one who controls the water will control the town," muttered Vihaan, catching on.

"We're almost ready to fire her up," said Klaus. "I wish that lady was here with her camera. . . ."

"Dude, you probably shattered her lens," joked Keeto. "I should be the new CMI spokesperson."

"Wait," said Hana. "We're getting ahead of ourselves. We still need to figure out some sort of filtration system."

"We also still need to eat lunch," said Keeto. "I'm starving."

"You're right," said Max. "Let's take a break. You guys have definitely earned one."

"Vihaan?" said Klaus, putting down his tools. "Where can we get some more of that spicy Indian spaghetti? That stuff is amazing, even if it is vegetarian."

Vihaan finally smiled. "I know a place nearby."

"Then what are we doing here?" said Keeto.

The entire team left the riverbank with Isabl. Charl stayed behind to guard the dissolved-air flotation device.

At the small restaurant Vihaan took them to, the spaghetti was spicy—with chili flakes and spices, like curry, whisked into the tomato sauce. Everyone was twirling their forks and digging in.

Except Max.

"Interesting," she said.

"You don't enjoy the spiciness?" asked Vihaan when he noticed that Max wasn't eating. She was just pushing her noodles around her plate.

"No. It's great. But look how the sauce seeps through the thinner noodle layers near the plate's perimeter but not through the thicker pile here at center."

"I guess," said Klaus, his mouth full of pasta.

"Spaghetti is a membrane," said Max, absentmindedly. "If you take this model to the logical extreme, you can densely pack the skinniest possible noodles together . . . and create a mesh that filters out the tiniest of particles."

"But," said Annika, mashing her noodles into a flat mat, soaking up sauce, "if our filter is soaking up all the impurities, it's eventually going to get clogged."

"Good point," said Vihaan. "How can we keep the filters clear, Max?"

She thought about that.

And then she thought about Einstein.

How he won his Nobel prize for his work on the photoelectric effect, which says that light shining on an object gives that object's electrons energy, causing them to spring off into the space surrounding it.

"Photocatalysis," said Max.

"You want to take photos of cat tails?" said Klaus.

"Brilliant," said Vihaan.

"Thanks," said Klaus.

"No, I mean the photocatalysis idea," Vihaan continued. "It takes Einstein's concept of the photoelectric effect but, in this case, the light shining on the object, the catalyst, gives electrons energy that drives chemical reactions."

"Titanium dioxide!" said Max.

"Indeed!" agreed Vihaan. "TiO_2, when activated by light, can break down pollutants into harmless little particles."

"And," said Annika, "if we harness the light we need from the sun, there's no extra energy cost."

"Our filtering problem is solved!" said Max.

"Hang on," said Isabl, touching her earpiece. "We have another problem. Down by the river. Charl says our two friends are back. And this time, they brought along a small army."

45

“We need to give those goons something else to worry about besides our water-cleaning machine!” Max shouted as her team tumbled into their transport van.

“What do you have in mind?” asked Isabl from behind the wheel.

Max, who was riding shotgun, spun around in her seat. “Vihaan?”

“Yes?”

“You say these packaged-water guys run the vending machines in town?”

“Indeed. Any machine labeled ‘Fresh & Pure.’ Those are theirs. The others belong to multinational—”

He was cut off by the van lurching forward. Isabl had just jammed her foot down on the gas.

“I saw one about a block from the river,” she said over the roar of the engine.

“Perfect,” said Max. “We’re going to make it malfunction. Big time. But first, we need to make one quick stop. A grocery store.”

“On it,” said Isabl, tapping the van’s navigation control panel, searching for the closest food market.

“You’re still hungry?” asked Keeto.

“No. We just need to pick up some salt, a newspaper, and a couple jugs of water. Fresh & Pure if they got it.”

“Now you want to buy their water?” said Annika. “I thought you wanted to attack their vending machines.”

“I do,” said Max with a mischievous grin. “Doing it with a jug of their own overpriced water will simply up the irony factor.”

Isabl squealed up to the curb in front of a small grocery shop. Max and Annika dashed in and grabbed the materials they needed for their science prank.

“Mix half a cup of salt for every two liters of water,” Max said when she returned to the van with the lukewarm water jugs.

Hana and Keeto took charge of making the salt water.

“You guys,” Max said to Toma and Klaus, “roll these newspapers into funnels. Annika? Hop in. We need to visit that vending machine.”

Max climbed back into the passenger seat. Isabl blasted off.

"Whoa!" shouted Keeto as the van banked through a sharp curve. "Slow down. You're sloshing the water."

"Deal with it!" Isabl shouted back as she slammed the van into another hairpin turn. "Time is of the essence. Charl says he can't hold them off much longer. There are six of them."

"Seriously?" said Klaus, rolling a sheaf of newsprint into a funnel tube. "I've seen Charl take on eight guys at once."

"These six all have guns," said Isabl.

"Oh. Okay. That's different."

"There!" shouted Annika, who was perched between the two front seats, scanning the horizon. "I see the vending machine."

Isabl fishtailed the van to a tire-screeching stop.

"Klaus?" said Max, jumping out of the van. "Give me your funnel. Hana? Hand me that jug of salt water."

"No," said Hana. "I'm coming with you."

"Fine. Let's run."

The two girls ran to the vending machine. "Shake up your solution," Max instructed Hana.

Hana jiggled her jug.

Max jammed the tip of the newspaper funnel into the vending machine's coin slot.

"Pour in the salt water," Max told Hana. "Straight down this tube."

"Seriously?" said Hana. "It'll go inside the vending machine."

"Exactly," said Max. "Inside, there's an electric switch that controls the release of the water bottles. The salt and water, mixed together, have created a mild electrical charge. When that solution washes over the switch, it'll create a salt bridge. Electricity will rush through it and short-circuit the machine, tripping the bottle-dispensing switch way faster than a fistful of coins."

"And the machine will start spitting out free bottled water?"

"Until it's completely empty," said Max.

"Woo-hoo!"

Hana poured in the water. Max heard something sizzle inside. Smelled a little ozone. Then she heard a *ka-thunk* followed by more *ka-thunk*s. Water bottles started tumbling out of the machine, bouncing onto the pavement, and rolling downhill.

People waiting in the water tanker truck line with buckets rushed over to grab the free bottles tumbling toward them.

Max and Hana raced back to the van.

"There's another Fresh & Pure vending machine two blocks that way," said Isabl, touching her ear. "But hang on. We may not need to hit it. Charl says the water goons just heard about their machine giving away free water. They're running up to fix it, leaving our bubble machine alone."

"Good," said Max. "So let's switch places with them!"

"On it," said Isabl. "Buckle up, everybody." She slammed her foot on the accelerator and shot off down the street toward the riverbank.

She had to lay on her horn to alert the six men running *up* the street to get out of her way.

The slowest man, the one at the back of the pack, was the one with the mustache.

Science has proven that smoking cigars will definitely make it harder for you to breathe and run at the same time. Especially in high altitudes.

46

After chasing away the bad guys, it took one more day for the team to add all the filtration equipment.

"It's time to turn this baby on!" cried Klaus.

Ms. James was on hand with her camera to document the big moment. A crowd of villagers had also gathered around the CMI team's dissolved-air flotation and filtering unit. Many were carrying jugs and buckets. Mr. Banerjee, Vihaan's grandfather, was standing with them, crossing his fingers, hoping his grandson's marvelous machine could help make his key man job a little less stressful.

"You guys ready?" asked Max.

"Ready!" shouted the rest of her team.

"Klaus? Flip the switch. Turn on the tap!"

Klaus braced his hand on the valve handle, then looked

directly into the lens of Ms. James's video camera. "This is one small flick of the wrist for man. One giant leap for clean water!"

Max had to laugh. Klaus, the CMI problem child, had turned into one of its most valuable (and entertaining) assets.

He cranked open the water valve. Vihaan and Annika flicked the switches that started sending highly pressurized bubbles fizzing through the "cleaning tank."

"We have sludge," reported Hana, as the first waste material was lifted up to the surface.

"Initiate skimming!" cried Keeto.

"Skimming," said Toma, punching a green button.

"Organic material is entering the gas mill," said Hana. "Commencing anaerobic digestion. We're breaking it down in our oxygen-free container. Pretty soon, we'll be cooking with our own gas!"

"And generating our own electricity!" added Toma.

"Filters are fully functional," said Annika, who was situated near the spigot at the far end of the unit. "We should have clean, potable water in ten, nine..."

Max and the others joined in the countdown as they watched the water working its way through the pipelines and "noodle" filters.

"...eight, seven, six, five..."

Max nudged Vihaan.

"You get the first drink," she said.

"Thank you."

". . . three, two, one!"

Vihaan turned the tap. Crystal-clear water flowed into his waiting tin cup.

"Quick," he said as the water rose up to the rim. "We don't want to waste a single drop of this. Who has a water jug they'd like to fill?"

The townspeople all stepped forward.

"I guess we better form a line," said Klaus, with a laugh.

And the people of Jitwan did. A very polite and orderly line.

When Vihaan's cup was full, an elderly lady at the head of the line placed a rubber bucket underneath the gurgling faucet. Ms. James's camera moved in for a close-up as Vihaan took a long, refreshing drink.

"Svaadisht!" he shouted. "Delicious!"

The crowd cheered.

The old lady who was waiting for her bucket to fill hugged Vihaan.

"Dhanyavaad!" she said.

"You are most welcome, Dadima."

"You vandals and hooligans!" The stubby man with the mustache and cigar was back. "You ruined one of our vending machines."

"Water is the driving force of all nature."

—Leonardo da Vinci

"Prove it, dude," said Keeto.

"Leave Jitwan!" growled the man, nearly biting his cigar in half.

"Not until we give these people the fresh, clean water they deserve!" declared Vihaan.

"That is dirty river water!" shouted the older water seller, waving his cane.

"Not anymore," said Max. "We cleaned it."

"We shall see about that!" The two men turned on their heels and walked away.

"Good-bye, Fresh & Pure water!" shouted a townsperson. "We don't need you anymore! We have Vihaan and his friends!"

"Vah!" shouted others.

"Hooray!"

Max was feeling fantastic. She and her team had found another solution to another problem.

But then Charl's satellite phone start buzzing.

He looked at the screen.

"It's a video call."

"Ben calling to congratulate us?" asked Max.

Charl shook his head. "No. It's Lenard. That robot we met in Ireland. He wants to talk to you."

47

Isabl motioned for the documentary maker to stop filming.

She did.

Max took the phone from Charl.

“Congratulations, Max,” said the grinning boy-bot, his face filling the phone’s screen. “My new friends in Jitwan tell me you have completed your water purification project. Well done. Now you are free to come work with me. We’re going to own the quantum computer world.”

“No, thanks.”

“But Dr. Zimm is here, too. He knows so, so much about you.” The automaton giggled. “I know some of it now, too. I must say, you have a very interesting history.”

“Where are you?”

"Very close to where you are."

"You're in India?"

"If that's where you are, Maxine, where else in the world would I want to be?"

"How'd you find us?"

"Through diligence and hard work."

Max glanced over at Klaus. He turned out his pockets. They were empty.

"I didn't get a new phone," he said. "I swear."

"Dude's been borrowing mine," added Keeto.

"It wasn't Klaus this time," said Lenard through the satellite phone. "That useful idiot has ceased being, well, useful. So, I did what I do better than any human being on the planet. I sifted through all available online data, and, believe me, there's a lot. So many sources for me to scan in a nanosecond. I am quite speedy, Maxine. Just imagine what we could do together. Now then, a pair of representatives from the Fresh & Pure water company will happily come escort you to my location."

"You're working with them?" said Max.

"Oh, yes. My creators, the Corp, recently acquired their water-packaging business. Therefore, they now work for us."

"Is Dr. Zimm with you?"

"Yes. But purely in an advisory capacity. He's here to answer all your questions. Who you are. Where you came from. I understand you are quite interested in ascertaining that information."

The offer, of course, was tempting. If Dr. Zimm really knew all he claimed to know, then Max might, finally, figure out... *everything*. Max had spent her whole life wondering who she was, where she came from, why her last name was Einstein. Dr. Zimm was the only person she'd ever met who promised to answer all those questions. Someone else could take over the lead at the CMI. Max could go back to her true mission: finding out who she was meant to be in this world.

Lenard must've read the look in Max's eyes. (She assumed the humanoid came equipped with the world's most advanced biometric sensors.)

"I'm so looking forward to collaborating with you and building the world's best, fastest, most artificially intelligent quantum computer, Maxine," it said. "It could become my new brain...."

Nobody called Max "Maxine." Except, of course, a machine that learned everything from databases and public records.

"Working with me is the next logical step on your

intellectual journey," Lenard continued, smirking broadly. "If you like, you can invite your Indian friend Vihaan to join us. I understand he has quite a grasp of quantum mechanics. He can be your assistant." Another giggle.

Max remembered something else Dr. Einstein once said: "It has become appallingly obvious that our technology has exceeded our humanity."

She didn't trust the high-tech nonhuman boy-bot. She didn't like him much, either.

And maybe who she was meant to be was who she was already being: the change she wished to see in the world.

"Sorry," she said to the phone. "The quantum computer can wait."

"But Dr. Zimm knows your birthday. . . ."

"Sweet. But I have more important things to worry about than when I should blow out candles or eat ice cream and cake."

"Really?" sniggered Lenard. "What could possibly be more important than discovering who you really are?"

"Oh, I don't know. Saving the world. Cleaning its water."

"Are you certain, Maxine?"

"One hundred percent."

"Fine. We will attempt to convince you to be more reasonable by other means."

"What other means?"

"You'll see. In precisely fifteen minutes. And Maxine? The next time you attempt to clean and purify river water, you might want to make certain your intake pipe isn't located downstream from a highly toxic copper smelting plant."

48

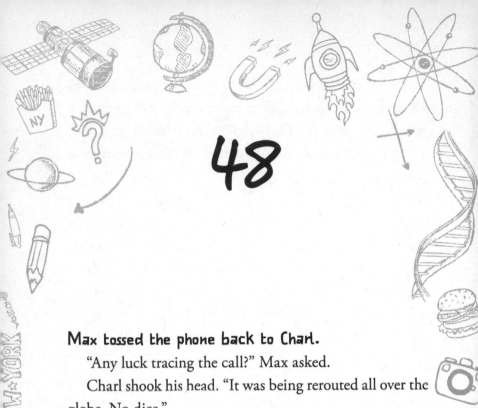

Max tossed the phone back to Charl.

"Any luck tracing the call?" Max asked.

Charl shook his head. "It was being rerouted all over the globe. No dice."

"This is awesome!" cried Ms. James, who was zooming in on the murky river. "You can see the pollution clouding the water! It's so swirly and orange, it looks like it's on fire!"

"That is not awesome!" Max shouted at the documentarian, who was starting to work her last nerve. She knew the damage pollution from a copper smelting plant could create. There'd be lead, arsenic, selenium in the water that would quickly contaminate the bodies of people living

downstream. The air pollution from a copper smelter was enough to kill leaves and make them fall off trees. Just imagine what might happen if you drank the stuff.

"What the Corp is doing is horrible!" Max screamed at the documentary maker.

"Maybe," said Ms. James. "But those swirls in the river make an awesome visual."

"I told you guys we should've moved on to some other project," whined Toma. "This is too dangerous. Like deep-void-of-space dangerous."

Max ignored Toma and ran over to the water-cleaning unit where Klaus and Annika were manning the controls.

"Shut it down," Max hollered. "Stop distributing water."

"But we just turned it on like two minutes ago!" moaned Klaus.

"It's too risky, Klaus. Shut it down!"

"Okay, okay..." Klaus flicked a series of switches.

Max turned to the line snaking up to the spigot, which Keeto had just twisted shut.

"Sorry, folks," she told the weary locals. "No more water today. The copper smelter upstream just dumped a load of arsenic and lead into the river. That's heavy duty, poisonous stuff."

"We know," said one of the women. "We remember

when the copper people polluted the air. Our throats burned."

"There was a choking fog," added a man.

Max wished she could promise these people that she could make things all better, the way other kids' mothers comforted them when they scraped a knee on the playground.

No one had ever made things all better for Max. She wondered if she could do it for Vihaan and everybody else who'd been counting on her.

"We'll fix this," Annika assured Max. "But we're going to need to run some serious tests to make one hundred percent certain those filters are doing their jobs and scrubbing the water clean!"

"We'll grab a sample," said Klaus. "I wish Tisa was here to help with the chemistry."

"Yeah," said Max, still lost in her thoughts. "Me, too."

"I can handle it," said Hana. "We botanists are all about making sure our plants are drinking clean water."

"Thanks," mumbled Max.

Hana started collecting water samples in stoppered test tubes.

Max finally looked to Vihaan. His shoulders were slumped. His eyes were moist with tears.

“This is horrible,” he muttered sadly. “We have done nothing but make matters worse.”

Max nodded. Vihaan was right. She was starting to question the whole mission of the Change Makers Institute. The only change they seemed to be making in Jitwan was to make things worse. Instead of helping clean up the water, their presence had made it even more poisonous.

Max and her team finished shutting down their dissolved-air flotation and filtering unit, then covered it with a heavy tarp. To Max, it looked like they were tucking it in and putting it to bed. Forever.

When they returned to the Royal Duke Hotel, there was an envelope waiting at the front desk.

It was addressed to “The Young Do-Gooders.”

“Let me open it,” said Charl, carefully inspecting the seams of the envelope for any trace of suspicious powder.

He sliced the envelope open with the blade of his tactical knife.

“What is it?” asked Max.

“An ultimatum,” said Charl.

“Is it from the Corp?” asked Klaus.

Charl nodded. “Our old friend. Dr. Zacchaeus Zimm.”

Max sighed. “What does it say?”

Charl read what Dr. Zimm had written: " 'Give us Max Einstein. If you do, your most recent pollution problems upstream will disappear. The rest of you can continue to attempt to save the world—just do it somewhere else. Ireland. Africa. Argentina. Rest assured that the water needs of Jitwan will be taken care of by the Fresh & Pure packaged-water company, a recently acquired and fully owned subsidiary of the Corp, Inc.' "

Nobody said much at dinner that night. Not even Keeto or Klaus.

Annika did point out the logic flaw in the Corp's argument. "How can we possibly continue to do good in the world if it means doing something so inherently evil? We can't turn Max over to Dr. Zimm."

Later, as Max tried to drift off to sleep, a task that seemed impossible, she had another, very short, internal conversation with her idol, Albert Einstein.

"I'm doing more harm here than good," she said.

"But remember, Max," replied the gentle, grandfatherly voice in her head, "the world will not be destroyed by those who do evil, but by those who watch them doing evil without doing anything themselves."

"Or it'll be destroyed by people like me," thought Max stubbornly. "The ones who do something that makes the world worse off than it was before they did it."

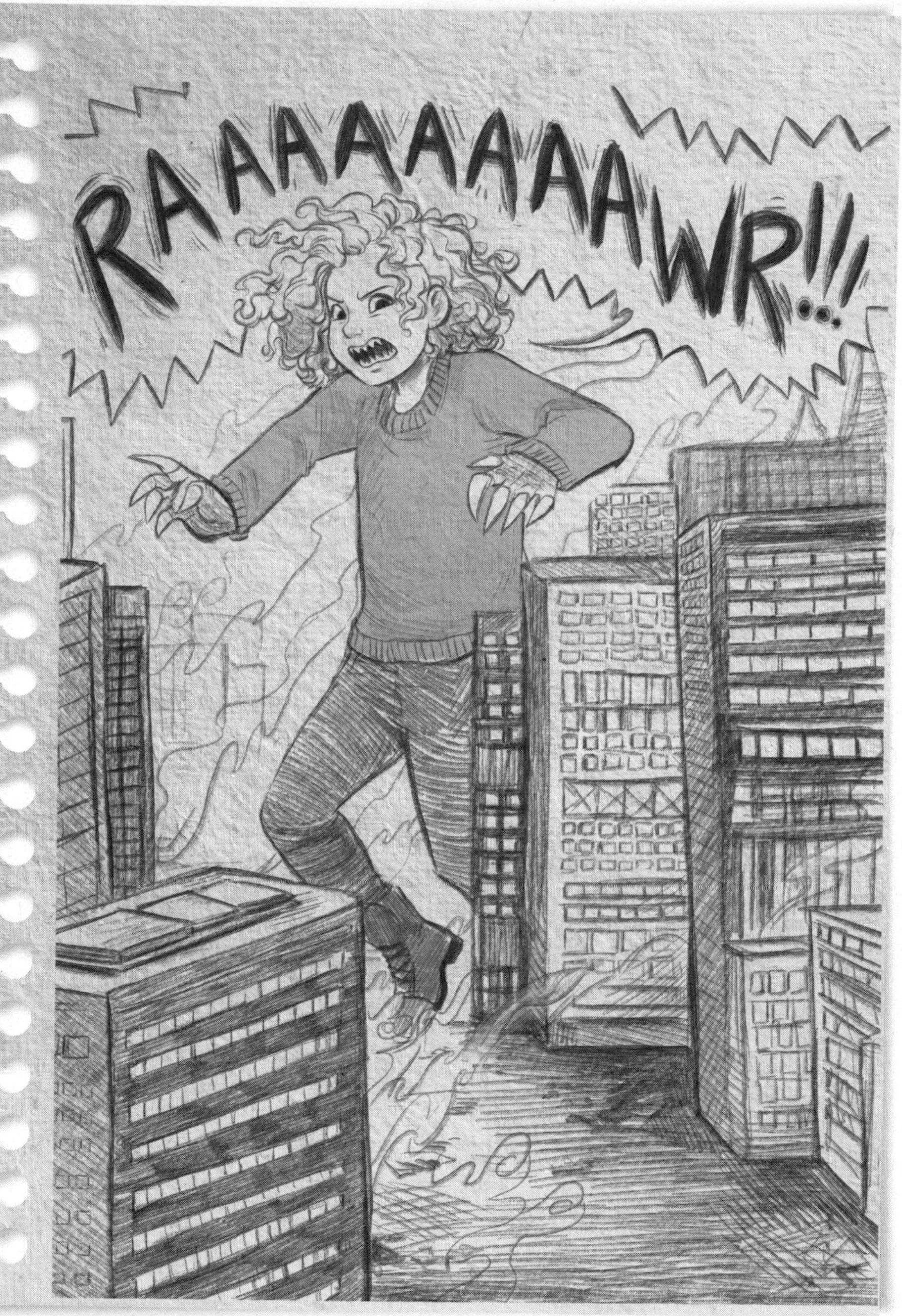
RAAAAAAAAWR!!!...

Her imaginary Einstein wanted to reply, but Max shut him down.

She'd made up her mind.

She knew what she had to do.

First thing in the morning, she'd call Ben. She'd tender her resignation as "the Chosen One."

She'd quit.

49

"Quit?" said Ben.

"Yeah," said Max. "I don't want to, but I think I have to."

It was early morning in India. Max had brought her secure satellite phone out to the dining hall deck where the reception was better.

"Look, Ben," Max continued, "my very presence is jeopardizing everything you and your Change Makers Institute are trying to do. You guys would be better off without me. I don't know why Dr. Zimm and the Corp want me so badly, but as long as I am leading the team, they will continue to sabotage your efforts."

"Because they're a bunch of bloomin' evil eejits!" cried a familiar voice.

Siobhan. She and Tisa came strolling out to join Max on the hotel's terrace.

"Um, Ben?" Max said into the phone.

"Yeah?"

"Siobhan and Tisa just showed up."

"I know. They finished the job in Ireland. Now they have a more important task: talking sense into you! Listen to your friends, Max. And remember what Dr. Einstein said."

"You mean that thing about how the world will not be destroyed by those who do evil, but by those who watch them without doing anything?"

"Okay," said Ben. "Sure. That one. Whatever works for you. Now, if you will excuse me, Klaus just sent a requisition for a ton of money so he can order all the parts you guys need to build more dissolved-air flotation and filtration units and clean even more water there in Jitwan."

Klaus should *be in charge,* Max thought. *He wants to keep going. Then again, he doesn't have Dr. Zimm and the Corp breathing down his neck.*

"So tell us, girl," said Tisa, the instant Max hung up the phone. "What's this we hear about you wanting to quit?"

"I just think it might be for the best...."

"Max?" said Siobhan. "Usually I admire your thinking and even your flight-of-fancy thought experiments. Truly,

I do. They're usually very entertaining. But right now? You're not thinking, girl. You're pouting and feeling sorry for yourself."

Max didn't have an answer. She knew Siobhan was right. That was the thing about friends. They sometimes knew you better than you knew yourself.

"By the way," said Tisa. "Hana shared her chemical analysis of the water post–pollution dump with me. Those noodle filters you guys came up with? They're doing the job, big time. They're brilliant, Max. The water is clean and potable."

"That means folks can drink it, right?" said Siobhan.

"Exactly," said Tisa with a nod.

"Then, crikey, just say it's 'drinkable,' not 'potable.' That makes it sound like you can carry it around. . . ."

Vihaan came out to the deck to join the group.

"The people of Jitwan are demanding that the local authorities deliver clean water," he said. "It's the people's right and the government's responsibility. We are going to stage a massive protest march and rally. We will shut down the copper smelter if we have to."

Max grinned. "You remind me of another brave Indian. Mahatma Gandhi. You're going to march on the copper plant the way he led the salt march to the sea to protest British colonial rule!"

Vihaan nodded. "Our personal heroes can teach us much, Max. Especially when we can emulate their actions and do like they did. However, we are not marching to the plant. We will take our civil disobedience to the municipal administrator's office and present evidence to expose that the water packagers are bribing officials so they can have easy access to tap water—water that is meant to flow into homes. Dada will speak up and testify, even if it means losing his job as a key man. Even if it means losing his life. Children like me will lead the march, for this is our world. We want it back."

Max once again understood why Ben wanted nothing but children (with a few well-armed chaperones) in his Change Makers Institute. Kids had the most to lose if changes weren't made, if big problems were ignored like adults had been doing for decades.

Siobhan looked Max in the eye. "Still want to quit, lassie?"

"No," said Max. "I want to do what *my* hero, Albert Einstein, would do. I want to stick with this problem until we find its solution!"

50

"We need to end the Corp's interference, once and for all," Max told her teammates. "If we can eliminate that problem, we'll be able to solve other problems much more easily all over the globe!"

"Good idea," said Siobhan. "But how exactly do you plan on defeating a nefarious, multinational organization with unlimited resources, not to mention a well-armed paramilitary force?"

All eyes were on Max.

"By giving them what they think they want, when, in fact, it might be exactly what *we* need."

The others just nodded. They had no idea what Max had in mind.

"She's doing that relativity thing again," Siobhan whispered to Tisa. "Ain't she? Where it all depends on how you look at something..."

"Yep," said Tisa. "Relativity to the max."

"I just hope whatever you are planning will stop the Corp from polluting the river or destroying our water filtration devices," said Vihaan.

"Oh, I think it will," said Max, who had run a quick thought experiment through her brain and hatched a clever new plan. "We need Keeto."

"To do what?" asked Vihaan.

To reconstruct a phone trace he did for us!"

"Why?" asked Tisa.

"So we can call Dr. Zacchaeus Zimm."

Keeto tapped keys on his laptop in rapid succession.

"I'm back-tracing the steps I took when you guys were in Ireland," he said. "The Corp had implanted a micro GPS tracking chip in Klaus's phone. It sent its reports to this number."

Keeto explained how the chip transmitted tracking and navigation data as well as the phone's communication activity.

"They were listening in on all your calls, dude," he told

Klaus. "They were tracking your text and internet activity, too."

Klaus looked sick—like he'd just eaten a sausage made out of rancid tube socks.

"Where did they transmit all that data?" asked Max.

"To a number linked to an application installed on a controlling device," said Keeto. "For instance, if you had an annoying humanoid robot..."

"Lenard," said Max. "He's better than a bloodhound."

"Actually," Klaus the robot expert explained, "Lenard is only as good as the information he receives. The thing operates on artificial intelligence. That means it, or, you know, *he,* only learns what the Corp wants it/him to learn. They fed my location information and communication details directly into its data stream because the Corp wanted Lenard to know everything he possibly could about me and us."

"Kind of creepy, huh?" said Keeto.

"Definitely," said Max.

While Max, Klaus, and Keeto reverse engineered how the Corp had tracked the team in Ireland, the other Change Makers (including Charl and Isabl) had gone with Vihaan, who was leading the Jitwan protesters. Years of pent-up frustration had definitely energized the locals. It reminded

Max of Newton's third law: For every action (political corruption leading to lack of drinkable water) there is an equal and opposite reaction (rage: citizens taking to the streets).

"We need to encourage the people of Jitwan to use the nonviolent resistance techniques of Mahatma Gandhi," Vihaan had told the group. "We will do as Gandhi did. We will boycott the Fresh & Pure water company, the way Gandhi had the Indian people boycott British goods in their quest for independence. We will urge the people to practice *ahimsa* at all times."

"Ahimsa?" Toma had asked. "What's that?"

"It means to 'not injure.' To show compassion. There will be no riots in the streets. Just a powerful show of nonviolent resistance."

The resistance by Vihaan and the people of Jitwan was only one part of Max's developing two-part plan.

"So, Keeto," she asked, "now that we know how to contact Lenard, can you hook me up with a spy cam of some sort?"

"Sure. I have a bunch in my bag."

"Why?" asked Klaus.

"Because, dude. *Because.* Here." Keeto handed Max a tiny device. "Poke it through a buttonhole on your shirt. Perfect."

"Thanks," said Max, making sure the miniature camera

lens looked like nothing more than a shiny button. "Now, let's jump back into Lenard's data stream. We need to re-establish contact with the humanoid."

"Sure," said Keeto with a shrug. "It'd be easy."

"What are you thinking, Max?" asked Klaus.

"That Keeto here is going to turn me over to the Corp."

"I am?" said Keeto. "Why?"

"Because the Corp is a super-secret organization. Nobody really knows that they exist. Right now, they're just some shadowy conspiracy theory."

"But," said Klaus, slowly catching on, "if you can record them admitting stuff on camera, we send it to all the major news organizations and make the Corp show its ugly face to the public—there goes their invisibility cloak. You can't be super-secret if everybody knows who you are."

"Exactly!" said Max.

"Keeto?" said Max. "When you contact Lenard, pretend to be a spy ready to turn me over to the Corp because you're jealous that you're not in charge of the Change Makers team."

"Are you?" asked Klaus. "Because, to be honest, I used to feel that way, too...."

Max ignored Klaus. "Make the call, Keeto."

"On it." Keeto put on his headset, tapped a series of numeric keys, and made the call.

We're gonna shine a light on The Corp!

Suddenly, Max felt a rush of warm air.

Someone had just stepped into the dining hall.

Actually, several someones. Dr. Zimm, several paramilitary personnel in Corp tactical gear, and Lenard.

"There's no need for your friend to contact me, Maxine," the humanoid said with a giggle. "Look! I'm already here."

51

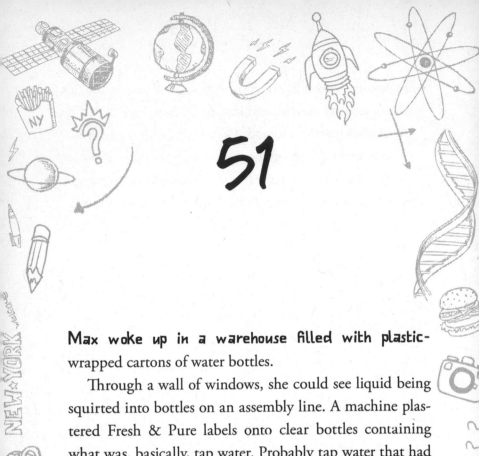

Max woke up in a warehouse filled with plastic-wrapped cartons of water bottles.

Through a wall of windows, she could see liquid being squirted into bottles on an assembly line. A machine plastered Fresh & Pure labels onto clear bottles containing what was, basically, tap water. Probably tap water that had been diverted from homes by key men under pressure from corrupt government officials.

Max found herself sitting, slumped in a chair. But her hands and ankles weren't bound or shackled to it. She felt groggy and vaguely remembered Dr. Zimm's thugs shooting her, Klaus, and Keeto with tranquilizer darts fired from air pistols. Dr. Zimm and Lenard must've figured

Max wouldn't need restraints. They were counting on the drowsy drugs to keep her under control.

That was their first mistake.

It took everything she had but, finally, Max was able to get to her feet and stumble over to the door. She gripped the knob. Tried to twist it. She couldn't. It was locked. Okay. They weren't as dumb as she originally thought.

However, they did make a second mistake.

Max still had her body cam.

Unfortunately, the LED indicator for the battery was blinking red. It was dead. There was no charge left. Keeto hadn't done a power check when he dug it out of his shoulder bag.

Max assumed the Corp goons had left the tranquilized Klaus and Keeto back at the hotel, lying on the floor. She also hypothesized that her friends' tranquilizers would be wearing off at about the same time as hers. Actually, she prayed that was the case.

Max looked up at the warehouse ceiling.

"Yes!" She saw what she was looking for: a battery-powered smoke detector.

She piled a stack of water bottle cartons directly underneath it. Then, she created a series of smaller carton towers to improvise a step stool. Body aching, she gingerly climbed

up each layer of cartons. Stretching out her hand until it felt like her shoulder would pop out of its socket, she snapped open the smoke detector. The door dangled on its hinge. Max took a deep breath, reached up again, got her fingers around the nine-volt battery, and yanked down hard.

She tugged it with everything she had because she needed to rip out the plastic cap connector with its wires, too.

"Got 'em," she said as she wobbled down her makeshift ladder. Her legs still weren't fully functional.

Moving as quickly as she could, Max forced open the back of the body cam to expose the dead battery. She slid it out of the unit. There was a roll of tape for sealing broken-open cartons sitting on a work table. Max tore off a few small squares. Next, she attached the stripped red wire from the nine-volt battery to the + symbol on the back of the camera battery. The black wire got taped to the - symbol.

Then Max waited.

For a full sixty seconds.

When the minute was up, she slid the recharged battery back into the body cam and flicked on its transmitter. The indicator light glowed green. She had battery power. Probably not much. Hopefully enough.

She panned the lens around the room.

"Okay, you guys," she whispered as her camera took in the warehouse and the automated conveyor belts out on the factory floor. “If you’re awake, I don’t know where they took me, but I think it might be a Fresh & Pure bottling plant. Or a warehouse. Does this thing do GPS coordinates? If so, you’re a bigger genius that I already realized, Keeto, and you know exactly where I am. Send Klaus. I think I’m gonna need him.”

The door clicked open.

Max whirled around.

Lenard had just shuffled into the room.

52

"Our new friends at the water company knew that you children were staying at the Royal Duke Hotel," said the smirking humanoid. "They simply forgot to inform us of that fact in a timely manner." The robot shook his head and seemed to sigh. "Unfortunately, my artificial intelligence is only as good as the data it is given."

That's when Lenard saw Max's miniature camera.

"Ah, very clever, Maxine."

Lenard was alone. No guards. No Dr. Zimm. No water company thugs.

"My friends didn't search you to see if you were carrying any concealed weapons or, in this instance, concealed cameras," the boy-bot said with a giggle. "Another human error committed by the ever-fallible Dr. Zacchaeus

Zimm. I assume that's a live feed, sending a signal to your compatriots?"

"Yep."

"Then I suppose we don't have much time, do we? Your friends will be here soon. The two mysterious adults with all the weaponry and martial arts training. Maybe even that annoying woman with the video camera. Meanwhile, I am here all alone. Everyone else had to head downtown to deal with your friend Vihaan and a mob of rather loud and unruly local protesters. Very well. I will make this quick. Dr. Zimm has much to tell you."

"About what?"

"All sorts of things. For instance, why you have that photograph of Albert Einstein in your suitcase. For that matter, let's talk about your suitcase. Do you know where they both came from?"

Max shook her head.

"Dr. Zimm gave you the suitcase *and* the photograph."

"What? Why?"

"Apparently so you'd always remember who you are."

"Okay—who am I?"

"We can discuss that later. After you agree to my terms."

"So, all of a sudden, *you're* in charge of the Corp's operations against the CMI?"

"Yes," said Lenard. "It's a much more efficient way to

operate because, as you might surmise, I am not prone to human errors."

Max knew she had to stall. She had to give Keeto and Klaus time to locate her. She had to act interested in Lenard's terms.

"Okay. I'm listening," she said. "What is it you want me to do?"

"Work with me. Redeem your hero, Albert Einstein."

Max laughed. "*Redeem* him?"

"Oh, yes. You see, Maxine, your beloved Dr. Einstein was from a different time and era. He made so, so many mistakes about quantum mechanics. Called it 'spooky action at a distance.' Couldn't stand how 'fuzzy' it was. Why, he even famously dismissed its uncertainty principle by saying that he doesn't believe God plays dice with the universe. Oh, he agreed that the math worked. He just couldn't wrap his nineteenth-century brain around what could become the shining scientific accomplishment of the twenty-first century."

"The Corp wants to build a quantum computer, right?"

"Yes, Maxine. One that can work on hugely complex problems by doing innumerable simultaneous computations. One that's small and compact. One that might even fit inside my head."

"You want a quantum computer brain?"

"Oh, yes. Even more than you want to know who your parents are. Work with me, Maxine, and, I project with ninety-nine percent certitude, that we will both find what we are searching for. You don't need the CMI. You've come as far as you can with them. But you and me? Working together? We will make quantum leaps! And Dr. Zimm will answer every single question that has ever kept you up at night! Who are you? Where did you come from? Why is your last name Einstein? Work with me, and Dr. Zimm will tell you everything he knows! Everything!"

53

Max considered Lenard's offer—for maybe two seconds.

When you're an orphan and suddenly find yourself part of a big family, you don't throw that away. The CMI was Max's first family. She would not desert them, not for all the secrets Dr. Zimm claimed to know.

But she still needed to buy time.

"Fine," she told Lenard. "How about we play a game of chess? If you can defeat me, I'll work with the Corp. If I win, you come work for me."

The robot laughed uncontrollably.

"Work for you?"

"And the CMI."

"Game on," chuckled Lenard. Then it pressed its ear

and a three-dimensional hologram of a chessboard was projected from a beam streaming out of its left nostril. The translucent, checkered board and thirty-two lined-up pieces hovered in the air between Max and Lenard.

"Just tap the piece you wish to move and swipe in the direction you wish to move it," Lenard explained. "Tap twice if you wish your pawn to move two spaces instead of one."

Max nodded and thought about the hundreds of times she'd defeated Mr. Weinstock (and everybody else) at the chess tables in New York City's Washington Square Park.

She was a chess master, for sure. But Lenard was an artificially intelligent robot. He probably knew even more grandmaster gambits and moves than Max did.

As they played, Lenard became somewhat chatty.

"So, if I may, Maxine, why do you and your friends strive to do good in the world?" he asked.

Max shrugged as she tapped a holographic bishop on the board. "I think we all have a duty to do as much good as we can. Besides, doing good feels good."

Lenard shook his head. "My views on charity are very simple," he said, sounding like he was quoting something his creators had downloaded onto his hard drive. "I do not consider charity a major virtue and, above all, I do not consider it a moral duty."

"And what do you consider a moral duty?" Max asked, making her move, threatening Lenard's king.

"Greed," he answered as he successfully defended against Max's strike. "Greed is good. Greed is right, greed works. Greed clarifies, cuts through, and captures the essence of the evolutionary spirit. Greed, in all of its forms—greed for life, money, love, and knowledge—has marked the upward surge of mankind."

Now he sounded like he was quoting a scene from a movie.

That's when Max fully realized that Lenard was just an empty vessel, bursting with whatever information and knowledge his minders pumped into him. In a way, Lenard was a lot like quantum physics. He could be simultaneously good and evil. It all depended on the information he received, the data he was given to mine.

Max slid her knight into the perfect pouncing position.

"Checkmate," said Max.

"Impossible. I am programmed to never lose."

"Yeah, that's the problem with programming. It comes from programmers and, unfortunately for you, they're human. Just like Dr. Zimm."

"I do not admit defeat. Winning isn't everything. It is the only thing."

"Who fed you all this gunk?"

“My friends at the Corp. They carefully curated my input. They gave me confidence. Swagger.”

“They gave you a bunch of garbage, too.”

Just then, the door creaked open.

Klaus.

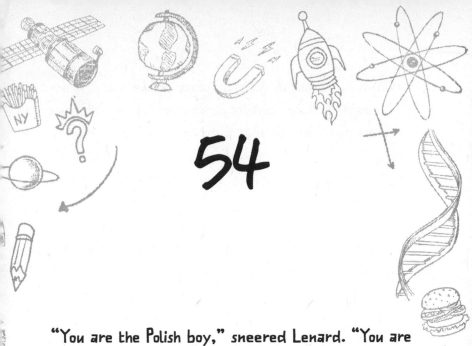

54

"You are the Polish boy," sneered Lenard. "You are Klaus. You were our useful idiot."

"That's right," said Klaus, sounding slightly sinister. "I see you've got Max. Good. You probably should've tied her to that chair. . . ."

"What are you doing here, Klaus?" asked Lenard.

"I want to be more than a useful idiot."

"Klaus?" said Max, sounding slightly scared. "What are you doing?"

"We've both always known that *I* should be the one heading up the CMI," said Klaus. "I think Ben has some kind of crush on you. That's why he chose you instead of me to lead the team. But you're right, Max. Your very presence slows us down. You're not cut out to be the top dog. I am."

Klaus slid a thumb drive out of his pocket.

"Lenard? I came here to upload some new information into your hard drive. All the data you might need to keep Max Einstein here under control. This is the good stuff. The dirt. Her likes, dislikes, and psychological weaknesses."

"Why did you bring this to me?" asked Lenard.

"Because I want what's rightfully mine. I want to eliminate my competition."

Now the boy-bot grinned. "You're a very greedy boy."

"Yeah," said Klaus. "Greed is good. So here. Let me hook you up. Dump some new Max Einstein–specific data into that amazing brain of yours. I see your USB input port. Just need to insert this thumb drive...."

Klaus moved behind the automaton. Into its blind spot.

"I am sorry, Klaus," said Lenard, attempting to twist his head around a full 180 degrees. He couldn't. "Data input can only be administered by authorized Corp technicians who have undergone—"

Klaus jabbed his thumb drive into the back of Lenard's head. The robot stopped talking mid-sentence.

"Don't worry," said Klaus. "I'm fully authorized. Heck, I'm a robotics genius!"

Lenard's head flopped forward. His eyes looked dead as a fish.

"Is he okay?" asked Max.

"Totally," said Klaus. "I just gave him a swift reboot. His hard drive is erasing itself. It'll take about an hour."

"Did anybody come with you?" Max asked.

"Charl. He came rushing back to the hotel ten seconds after Keeto and I woke up and contacted him. He's out in the hall. Crouching below that window there. He's my personal security detail. It's pretty cool."

"Is Keeto okay?" asked Max.

"Yeah. After Charl and I were good to go, he headed down the hill to join Vihaan's protest rally." Klaus rapped his knuckles on the window. "Olly, olly, oxen free! It's safe to come in. The robot is in sleep mode."

Charl popped up and bustled into the room.

"This facility is clear," he reported. "Dr. Zimm, the Corp mercenaries, and the packaged-water company's enforcers are all in Jitwan, trying to do something that will make Vihaan's nonviolent protest turn violent. You and Lenard were the only ones in this building, Max."

"The robot wanted to deal with you one-on-one," said Klaus, gesturing toward the mechanical mannequin, which was now slumped over at the waist. "Probably figured it could use its treasure trove of pure logic to turn you against us. We might've deserved it, too. Especially me."

"Impossible," said Max with a grin.

"Are you forgetting how I goofed up with that phone Dr. Zimm sent me?" said Klaus.

"You made a couple mistakes," Max told him. "So what? It's like Einstein always said: 'Anyone who never made a mistake never tried anything new.' "

"Albert Einstein said that?"

"Nope," Max said with a grin. "*Max* Einstein said that. Speaking of trying something new..."

"What?" said Klaus. "I see that look in your eye, Max. That's the *aha* glint you get right before you have a great big brainstorm."

Max turned to Charl. "We need to transport Klaus and Lenard to CMI headquarters in Jerusalem."

"You want to steal their robot?" said Klaus.

"It's not really stealing. It's...refurbishing. Plus, that was our deal."

"Huh?"

"The stakes of our chess game. If I lost, I'd go work for the Corp. If Lenard lost..."

"He'd work for us?" said Charl.

"Yep. So now we need you, Klaus, to head up our CMI robotic restoration. We need you to give Lenard's artificial intelligence some new raw data to chew on. The poor guy's bionic brain needs better material."

"Sounds like a plan to me," said Klaus.

"Is everybody else still at the protest?" Max asked Charl.

Charl nodded. "Vihaan and his grandfather are leading the march through the streets, winding their way to the municipal commissioner's office."

"I'll go join them," said Max. "You help Klaus haul our new friend Lenard out of here."

"Put us on the first flight to Jerusalem, Charl," said Klaus. "I've got some major robo-rebooting to do."

55

Max joined the rest of the CMI team and what looked like the entire population of Jitwan holding a rally in the square outside the municipal commissioner's office.

Vihaan and his grandfather were leading the rally, which, Max figured, was as it should be. This was their home. Their country. A lot of the marchers were children. They were out in the streets, fighting for their future.

"I am a key man!" cried Vihaan's grandfather through a bullhorn. "The water barons bribe the police! Water should belong to all the people, not just the greedy ones with the money to make it flow where they wish!"

"We will continue to clean your water!" added Vihaan, taking the bullhorn from his grandfather. "My Change Maker friends and I will build more machines. We will

Gandhi's Theory of Nonviolent Protest in Action.

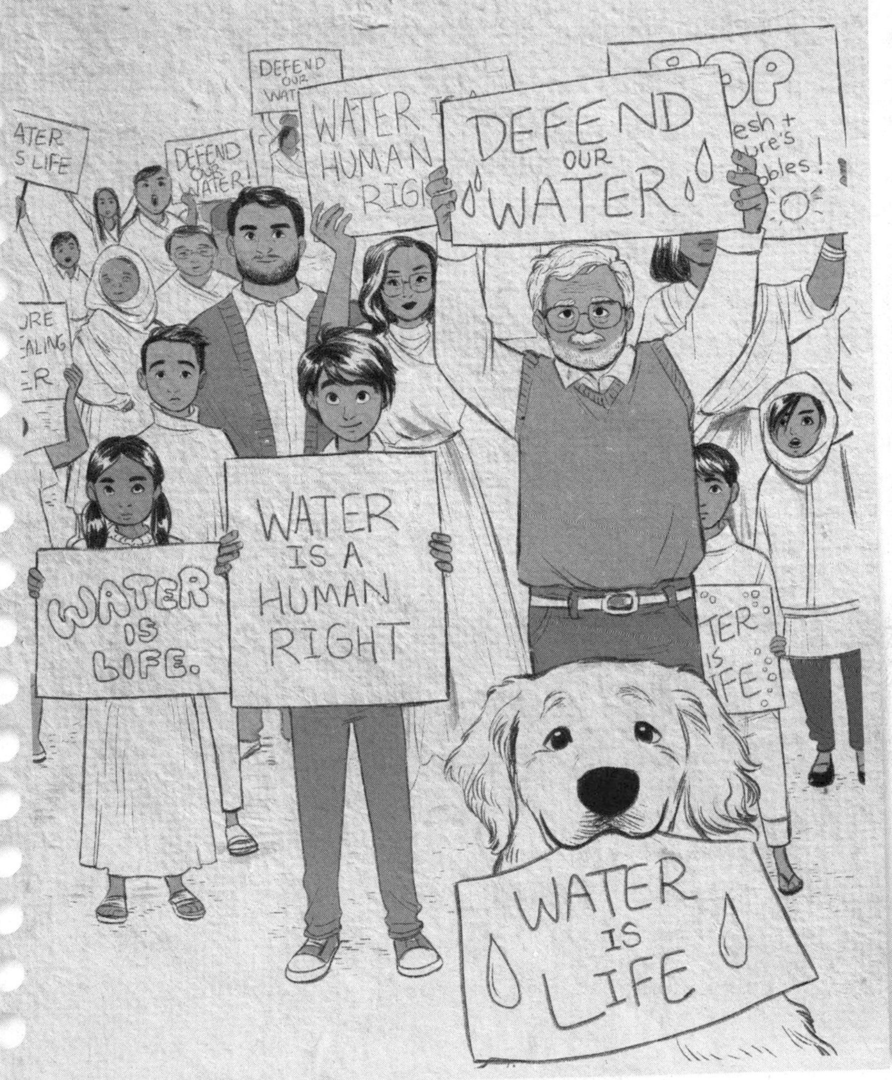

teach you how to operate them. But it is up to you, the people of Jitwan, to make the real changes. It is up to you to make certain the government ensures that the clean water goes to those who need it most. Not to those who pay the most so they can put our filtered water into bottles and bags and sell it for a profit!"

A small man who looked like a mayor came out to the steps of the government building to address the crowd.

"We will make many changes," the municipal commissioner promised Vihaan and the protesters. "Starting with firing the police officers who were supposed to protect our key men but, instead, intimidated them into *not* doing their duty. I've also asked the police to arrest several representatives of the Fresh & Pure water company. They have much to answer for."

The crowd cheered. Max figured the two thugs from the water company would be spending the night in jail.

"This is the dawn of a new day!" the commissioner promised. "Thanks to Vihaan Banerjee and his young friends, we will soon have many new sources of clean water. We will make certain that it gets where you, the people, need it most."

The crowd cheered again. If elections were held that afternoon, the municipal commissioner would've won in a landslide.

"Thanks for sending Klaus to answer my distress signal," Max said to Keeto when she found him carrying a WATER IS LIFE placard in the crowd.

"No problemo. I tweaked out that camera to record the GPS coordinates of every shot it recorded. Finding you was easy."

"Only because you made it easy. You're a genius."

Keeto shrugged. "What can I say? It's a gift. And Max?"

"Yeah?"

"Everybody on our team is a genius, remember?"

"Yep. And I'll never forget it."

"Your friend Dr. Zimm just took off," Siobhan told Max when she came over. Tisa was with her. "We've been keeping an eye on him and his goons."

"They heard what the commissioner said and decided it was time to tuck in their tails and scurry back under whatever rock they climbed out from," added Siobhan.

"I wouldn't be surprised if the Corp sold its stake in the Fresh & Pure water company," said Tisa, "seeing how it's become a public relations disaster."

"I did hear Dr. Zimm tell his troops that they needed to go back to the warehouse to pick up a 'piece of equipment,'" said Siobhan.

"Lenard," said Max.

"Exactly."

"Oops," Max said with her own giggle.

"What?"

"Lenard is gone. He's on his way to CMI headquarters in Jerusalem with Klaus. He's not a bad robot, you guys. He was just programmed that way."

"So, we're going to counter-program the genius menace?" said Tisa. "We're going to make sure his artificial intelligence is filled with smarter, better ideas?"

"Not us," said Max. "Klaus."

"Crikey," said Siobhan. "The bloomin' bot is going to want to eat sausages all day, every day."

Max and her friends laughed.

It felt great.

To laugh.

And to have friends.

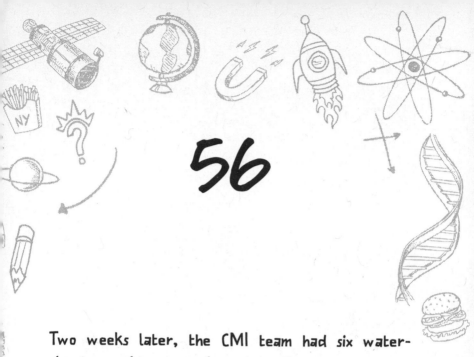

56

Two weeks later, the CMI team had six water-cleaning machines up and running in Jitwan.

They were all self-sufficient and green—manufacturing their own electricity by using the waste products skimmed off the top of the bubble tanks to create gas to power their self-contained generators.

Max was super proud of her team. Yes, they were young, but they had already accomplished so much. They'd brought electricity to the Congo and, now, clean water to Jitwan.

And there was so much more to do.

"I wish Jitwan had a better infrastructure to deliver our freshly cleaned water," said Vihaan. "The underground water pipes are antiques, left over from the days of British colonial rule. To replace them would cost a fortune."

"Truly novel ideas emerge only in one's youth. Later on, one becomes more experienced, famous — and foolish." —Albert Einstein

"I'll talk to Ben," said Max. "Maybe he could help out with an interest-free loan."

Keeto posted all the CMI plans for cleaning water on the internet so towns and villages all over India (not to mention all over the world) could copy what had been done in Jitwan.

"This is how we make big-time change," said Max. "We find a problem, we work with it until we come up with a solution, and then we test out that solution on a small scale."

"And once we prove that it works," said Annika, "the next logical step is to share it with the world."

"For free!" added Toma.

"Yep," said Max. "I think that's why the Corp hates us. They don't understand the word 'free.' They like another R-E-E word better: greed!"

"So, what's our next problem in need of a solution, Max?" asked Hana. "Where do we go next?"

"I'm not sure," said Max. "I have all sorts of ideas, of course, but I think I need to talk them over with Ben."

As if on cue, her satellite phone started buzzing.

It was a call from Ben.

He quickly agreed to the loan idea. Then he said he wanted to meet Max.

Right away.

In London.

57

"When you're done in London, come back to visit us up in Ireland," Siobhan told Max as they packed up their suitcases in the hotel.

"I might do that," said Max.

Max had added a new souvenir to her suitcase collection of Einstein memorabilia: a copy of a photograph that Vihaan had given her, showing Mahatma Gandhi and Albert Einstein together.

The quote Vihaan had written on the back of the photo meant a lot to Max, too.

I believe that Gandhi's views were the most enlightened among all of the political men of our time. We should strive to do things in his spirit; not to use violence

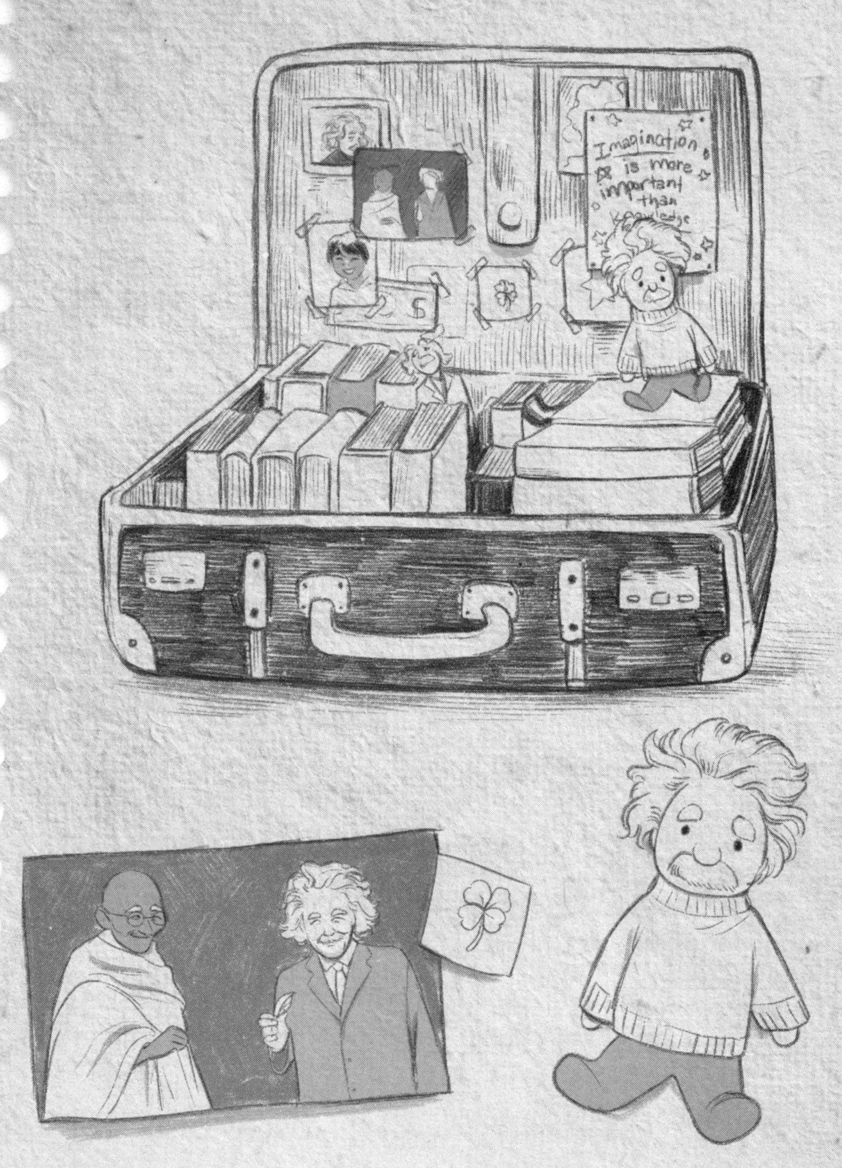
Imagination
is more
important
than

in fighting for our cause, but by non-participation in what we believe is evil.

—Albert Einstein

Max agreed. She would not participate in anything she believed was evil.

She would not build a quantum computer for the Corp, no matter how much information about who she was and where she came from Dr. Zimm promised her.

Max flew to London with Isabl. She felt right at home in the foggy city. A lot of people were bustling around in floppy trench coats, just like hers. Max hoped to see some of the tourist sites. The London Eye Ferris wheel. The Science Museum. Buckingham Palace.

But Ben had other plans.

"I wonder why he wants us to meet him at this obscure restaurant," said Isabl when she received a text with further instructions.

"He's Ben," said Max with a shrug. "He's quirky."

"I wonder if you'll be living in London now?" Isabl asked.

"Maybe. I'm not sure."

"It must be difficult not having a home."

"It was," said Max. "But now, I do have a home. The CMI. Wherever we go, that's my home."

Ben had asked to meet Max and Isabl at a place called

Kitchin N1 at 8 Caledonia Street in the Kings Cross district of London.

Max did a quick internet search and discovered it was a two-hundred-plus seat Chinese-Thai-Indian-Italian fusion restaurant with an "all you can eat" buffet—everything from pizza to tandoori to fish to Chinese noodles.

"That's a lot of food," Max mumbled. "And you can eat all you want for one price."

"Good thing I'm hungry," added Isabl.

They found Ben seated at a table not far from a cascading fondue fountain gurgling with thick brown chocolate.

"Uh, hello, Max. Isabl."

"Hi, Ben," said Max. She was glad to see the young billionaire again.

"Good job in, you know, India."

"Thanks."

"So, Ben?" asked Isabl. "When did you start going to restaurants with all-you-can-eat buffets?"

"Today, I think. Yes. Today. This is my first time. Look at all that food." He gestured toward the noodle bar and the tandoori oven. "They have garlic naan, plain naan, peshwari naan. . . ."

Naan was the warm and puffy Indian bread that Max had loved in Jitwan.

"They have chicken tikka, French fries, crispy duck . . .

food from all over the world. They have desserts. Crème brûlée, apple crumble, chocolate fondue. And you can eat as much as you like—of anything and everything."

"Oh-kay," said Max. "I guess we're in for a royal feast."

"Good," said Isabl. "We didn't eat on the plane. I'm starving."

"Ah," said Ben. "You're hungry. Just like 795 million other humans on the planet today. That's about one in every nine people. This year, 36 million of those same people will die from hunger."

Max pushed back from the table. "All of a sudden, I don't feel so good about having dinner at an all-you-can-eat buffet."

"Me, neither," added Isabl, taking her napkin out of her lap and wadding it up into a crumpled cloth ball.

"Don't just feel bad," said Ben. "Let's do something about it."

"Is this our next mission?" asked Max. "World hunger is a major problem."

"It's huge," said Ben. "But if anybody can solve it, you guys can!"

"Well," said Max, "we know we can't solve problems with the same thinking we used when we created them. We'll need some new ideas. New thinking."

"You may also need a new CMI teammate." Ben stood up from the table. "He's waiting for us in the parking lot."

"You've recruited and trained a new member?" said Isabl as she and Max followed Ben out of the restaurant.

"Yes," said Ben. "He's a very good thinker. Knows how to work data like no one I've ever met."

Ben led Max and Isabl to a tall van parked behind the restaurant. He rapped his knuckles on the rear doors. They swung open.

"Hey, Max. Hello, Isabl." Klaus was in the van, munching on tiny sausages he plucked from a tin can. "Meet Leo."

He gestured toward the humanoid robot formerly known as Lenard.

"Hello, Max. Hello, martial arts lady. . . ."

"Her name is Isabl," Klaus told the robot.

"Correction. Hello, Isabl."

"Uh, hi, Leo."

"Did you reprogram him?" Max asked Klaus.

"Yep. Followed your specifications as best I could. Added a few data points of my own."

"Max," said the boy-bot, "I look forward to working with you and your team. Your friend Klaus has filled my head with all sorts of fascinating new information, including several tasty sausage recipes from around the globe."

Max laughed and shook her head. "You couldn't resist, could you?"

"Nope," said Klaus. "But I fed him all your good stuff, too."

"Man would indeed be in a poor way if he had to be restrained by fear of punishment," said Leo.

"Albert Einstein said that," remarked Max.

"Yep," said Klaus. "I figured a few quotes from Dr. Einstein might help permanently erase all that junk the Corp was feeding him. So I downloaded a complete digital copy of a book called *The Ultimate Quotable Einstein*. Now, you and Leo can swap quotations all day long."

Max nodded and turned to Leo. "What about greed? Making money?"

"Well, Max, if I may offer some sage advice: Try not to become a person of success but rather try to become a person of value."

Max smiled. "Dr. Einstein couldn't've said it better himself. Welcome to the team, Leo."

"Thank you," said the smiling robot.

And then, it giggled.

"Yeah," said Klaus. "That was one glitch I just couldn't code out of him."

What would Max do?

Read on for fun activities and experiments you can do yourself!

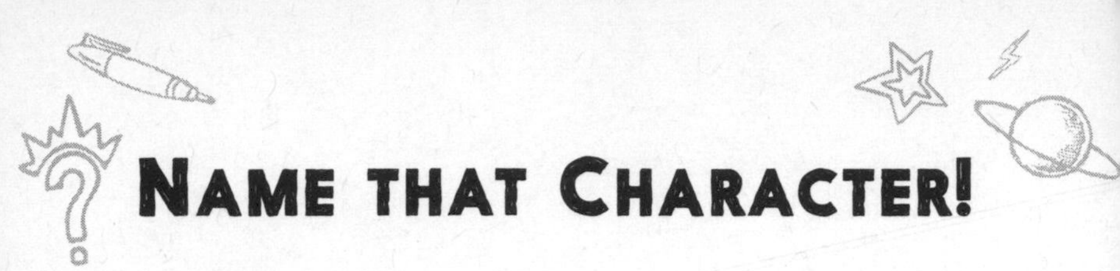

Name that Character!

Max has some really special people in her life! Each one of them has unique qualities, thoughts, or expertise that makes them who they are. Below, you will find clues that are specific to one of her teammates at the Change Makers Institute. Unscramble the letters to find the name of the character.

Robotics expert; from Poland; loves all kinds of food.	uakls
A biochemist from Kenya; earned a doctorate at the age of 13.	aist
Expert in geoscience; hopes one day to develop technology that can predict major natural events.	oiahsnb
From California; computer scientist and expert hacker who studied at Stanford University.	eoekt
14-year-old billionaire; set up the Change Makers Institute.	enb
"We must be the change we wish to see in the world."	iahdng

"The only sure way to avoid making mistakes is to have no new ideas." **iieennts**

13 years old; PhD in quantum mechanics. **iaahvn**

Considered a "master of formal logic." She helped Max escape from the Corp in Jerusalem. **aainnk**

Botanist from Japan; passionate about water conservation. **aanh**

Astrophysicist; from China; obsessed with black holes, dark matter, and wormholes. **oatm**

Who are some special people in your life? Create your own clues and scramble their names. Pass them along to a friend or family member to solve!

Answers: Klaus, Tisa, Siobhan, Keeto, Ben, Ghandi; Einstein, Vihaan, Annika, Hana, Toma.

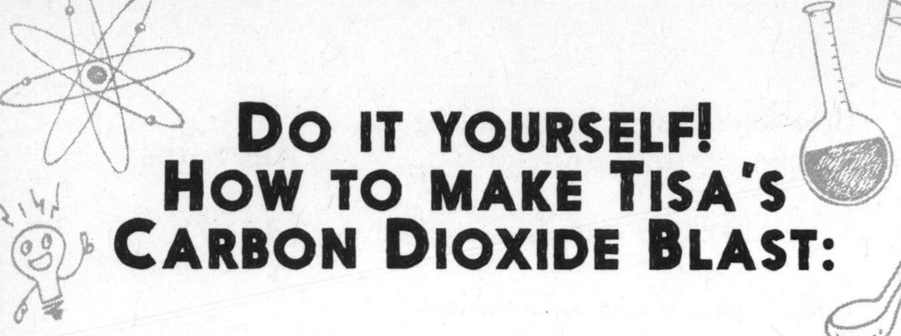

DO IT YOURSELF! HOW TO MAKE TISA'S CARBON DIOXIDE BLAST:

Materials:

2 tall cups

Water

Baking Soda

Dish Soap

Vinegar

Parental supervision advised.

Instructions:

1. Pour water into cup until it's about a third full.
2. Add two spoonfuls of baking soda.
3. Fill a separate cup with vinegar and a squirt of dish soap. Mix well.
4. Quickly pour the vinegar mixture into the cup of water.

5. Stand back and watch the eruption!
6. Add more vinegar to repeat the reaction until the baking soda mixture is gone.

How It Works

When they come into contact, vinegar and baking soda react and form a gas called carbon dioxide (CO_2). The carbon dioxide gas surges upward through the mixture, causing it to foam up and expand out of the cup. Awesome!

Time to Experiment

Repeat the process a few times, but with small differences each time. Record your findings so that you can remember the best way to achieve maximum blast!

- Skip the dish soap. Is there a difference?
- Try adding one spoonful fewer of baking soda. What happens?
- What if you added the dish soap to the baking soda mixture instead?
- What other variations can you think of? Try them all!

Where in the World is Max Einstein?

Max travels throughout the book (again!) working with the Change Makers Institute (CMI) to help those in need. Dr. Zimm is hot on Max's trail to stop her good deeds and kidnap her so that he can use her knowledge for his own greed! Solve the clues to find out where Max went to escape the clutches of Dr. Zimm. You may need to use your book to help with these clues.

Destination 1

Where in the world is Max?

1	2	3

4	5	6	7

Max got up bright and early to teach her Physics 1601 class. You can find her on the 3rd floor in Pupin Hall. Where is Max? (p. 28)

___ [___ 5] ___ ___ ___ ___ ___ ___

___ [___ 1] ___ ___ [___ 2] [___ 6] ___ ___ ___ [___ 4]

It always helps Max to unwind at the end of a long day. She stopped here to play some chess with Mr. Weinstock. Where is Max? (p. 16)

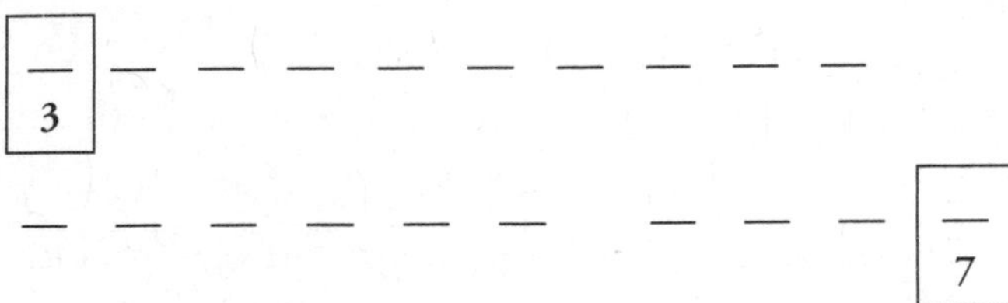

Destination 2

Where in the world is Max?

1	2	3	4	5	6	7

Max was hungry for some fish and chips. She stopped here to eat. Where is Max? (p. 107)

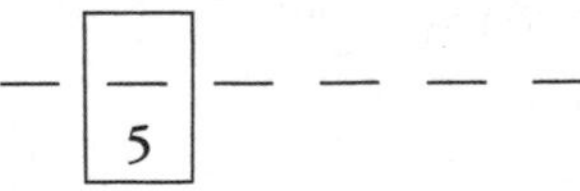

This hilly region is home to three S's—Siobhan, sausages, and sheep. Where is Max? (p.109)

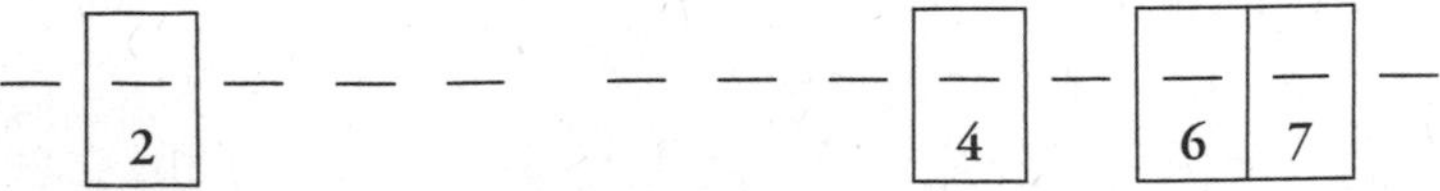

Klaus told Max she had to come here to try shepherd's pie, herbed beef pastries, and an enormous bowl of beef stew. Where is Max? (p. 133)

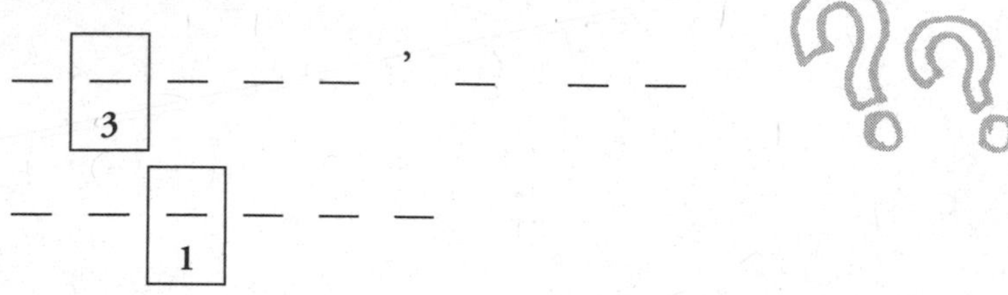

DESTINATION 3

Where in the world is Max?

1	2	3	4	5

Max paused from saving the world to take in the view here. She saw crowded hillsides and a town with brightly colored three- to four-story buildings. Where is Max? (p. 171)

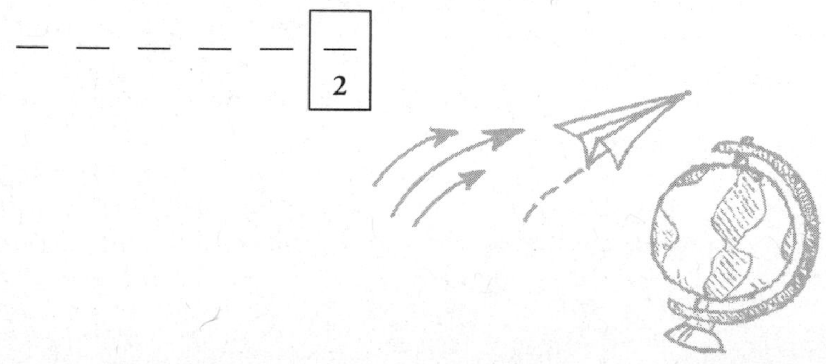

Max wanted to check on the bubble contraption they made for the people of Jitwan. Where is Max? (p. 217)

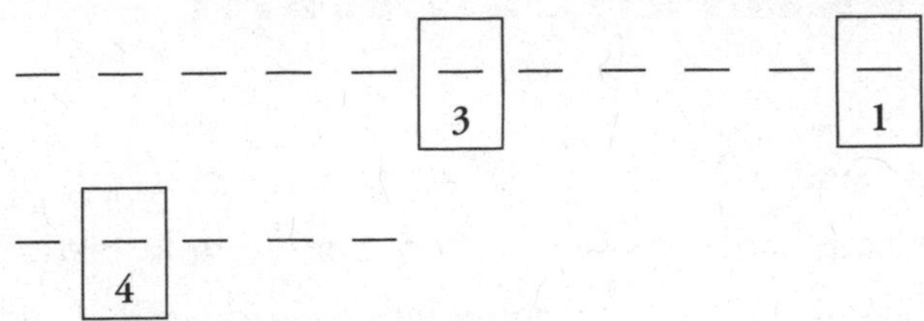

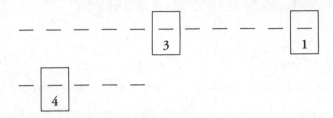

Max woke up in this building after she was shot with a tranquilizer dart. Where is Max? (p. 256)

Answer:
NEW YORK 1. Columbia University 2. Washington Square Park
IRELAND 1. Galway 2. Irish Midlands 3. Leavy's of Foigha
INDIA 1. Jitwan 2. Narmadavari River 3. Warehouse

Action/Reaction Scavenger Hunt

Max (and Newton!) have taught us that for every action there is an equal and opposite reaction. For example, picture yourself kicking a ball. Your foot swings toward the ball and makes contact—the action. Then the ball moves away with a similar amount of force and speed—that's the reaction.

Max wants your help in preparation for her next lecture. She needs to find everyday examples of Newton's 3rd Law. For this activity, you are going on a scavenger hunt to find examples of Newton's 3rd Law in the world around you. You will have to figure out the action and reaction. Put on your walking shoes, grab your *Max Einstein: Rebels with a Cause* book, a pencil and paper, and head out into the world (or your neighborhood)!

1. Look up into the sky. Is it a bird, a plane, or Superman? IT'S A BIRD! Watch as the bird floats high above you. The wings of the bird are pushing air down, which is the action. That causes the bird to fly up in the air, which is the reaction.

2. Find a balloon. Take a deep breath...blow into it. Now, when the balloon is good and full…let go! The air coming out of the balloon is the action. The balloon moving rapidly is the reaction.

Now it's your turn to find more examples. Here are some to get you started. What is the action? How about the reaction? Fill out the chart to finish the Scavenger Hunt. Good luck!

- o **Blowing on a candle**
- o **Swinging a bat at a baseball**
- o **Dropping a book on the table**
- o **Touching a soap bubble**
- o **Pedaling a bicycle**
- o **Bouncing a ball**

Example of Newton's 3rd Law	Action	Reaction
Bird flying in the air.	The wings are pushing the air down.	The bird going up in the air.
Balloon	Air coming out of the balloon.	Balloon moving.

A Speedy Escape

Max will not go anywhere without her suitcase containing all of her precious Albert Einstein items. It is the first item she always makes sure to have! Within her suitcase, you will find an Einstein doll, pictures, and other memorabilia. Imagine you were being chased by an evil scientist like Dr. Zimm and only had enough time to grab your suitcase and escape to a new place. What would you pack in your suitcase? Draw the items in the suitcase that are important to you.

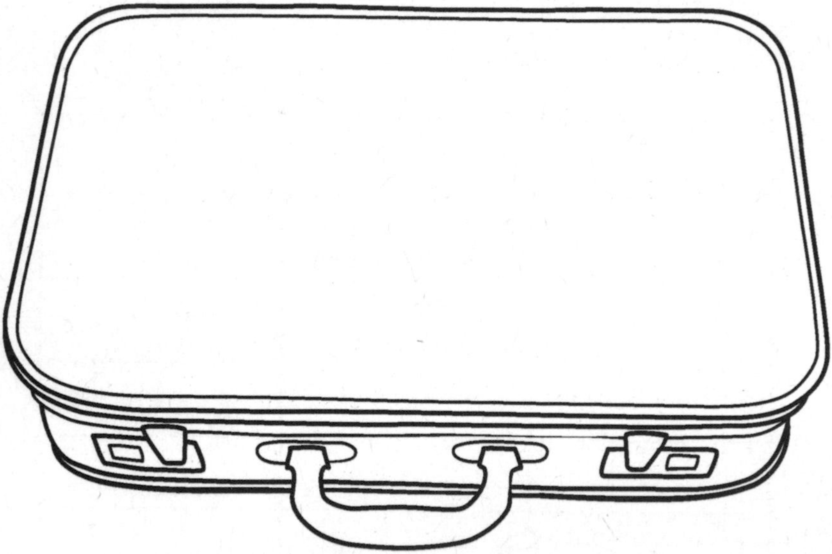

Max's Notebook

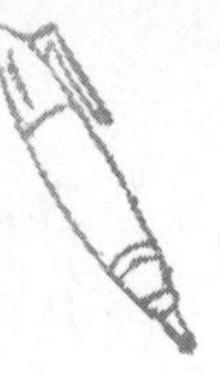

Newton's Laws of Motion

When Sir Isaac Newton was bonked on the head with an apple it gave him a knot but also a big idea! He came up with three rules to explain how objects behave in motion:

1st Law: an object at rest tends to stay at rest, and an object in motion tends to stay in motion. Like when you're riding a bike! If the bike is in motion, you can coast without pedaling. But if the bike is at rest (not moving), it'll stay that way until you give it a push.

2nd Law: the more force you put on an object the faster it moves. But if you put the same amount of force on a bigger object, it will move slower. For example, if you push Albert Einstein on a swing, he will swing a lot slower than if you push me, Max, because grown-up Albert is a lot bigger (more mass). Force = Mass x Acceleration.

3rd Law: for every action there is an equal and opposite reaction. Okay, let's do an experiment. Stand up and push on the ground with your legs. You jumped in the air, right? That's because the force you applied to the ground also propelled you into the air.

Theory of Relativity

This is my favorite Albert Einstein theory—but you probably already knew that! It's actually two theories: One is called "special" relativity and the other is called "general" relativity.

Special Relativity

Scientists discovered that light is really cool and weird—it doesn't act like *anything* else in the universe. No matter how fast you move and no matter what direction you go, *the speed of light is always the same*. This was very confusing to scientists, and it took Albert Einstein to figure out how this could be true: It's only possible if time slows down!

Scientists call this *time dilation.* Whether you're riding a horse, driving a race car, or piloting a fighter jet—you measure the speed of light to be exactly the same. So time must move slower the faster you move! That's why astronauts on the International Space Station, who are zooming around the Earth at 5 miles per second, age slower than people on Earth. Whoa.

General Relativity

Einstein's other theory of relativity says that gravity (the powerful force that keeps us on planet Earth and not floating into space) and inertia (an object in motion tends to stay in motion) are pretty much the same. For instance, when an airplane speeds down the runway, the inertia pushes you against your seat in a way that feels just like gravity. This is why future spacecraft designs often have large spinning cylinders attached to them—it's manufactured gravity for astronauts. Heavy stuff.

Photoelectric effect

A photon is a bundle of electromagnetic energy. It is the basic unit that makes up all light. In some cases, a photon can be absorbed by stuff (scientists call it matter) and the result is extra energy released as heat. Have you ever walked barefoot on pavement? Hot, hot, hot! That's because blacktop absorbs the sun's rays (i.e. photons) and releases heat.

Sometimes, when photons interact with matter, it can release electrons, and this is called the photoelectric effect. That's how the solar panels we installed in the Congo are able to convert light into electricity. Albert Einstein won the Nobel Prize in 1921 for his explanation of the photoelectric effect. I think the Change Makers should win a Nobel Prize in friendship!

Select content was created by Room 228 Educational Consulting, with public school teacher Michelle Assaad as lead teacher.

Be the Change!

Max is asked to be a part of a very special team—the Change Makers Institute (CMI). The purpose of CMI is "to make significant changes to save this planet and the humans who inhabit it." Now it is your turn to make a difference. Create your own Change Makers Club in your school or community!

- ❏ Gather a group of kids who are interested in making change. Remember to create a team like Max did where everyone brings a different skill to the club.

- ❏ Find an adult to be an advisor or helper for your club.

- ❏ With your club, think about a change you would like to make in your school or community to help improve it in some way. Try some Thought Experiments to get those brainstorms going! For example, create a program to reduce bullying in your school.

- ❏ Make a plan! Some things to think about...
- ❏ What role will each person take? (What roles existed on Max's team? What personalities fit each role? Something to think about!)
- ❏ Who are the people you need to talk with to move your plan along?
- ❏ What materials will you need?
- ❏ Put your idea into action and make that change!
- ❏ Don't stop there...reflect on what went well and what didn't. Remember, even Albert Einstein made mistakes! Make those changes and plan your next problem to solve with your new Change Makers Club!

About the Authors

James Patterson received the Literarian Award for Outstanding Service to the American Literary Community from the National Book Foundation. He holds the Guinness World Record for the most #1 *New York Times* bestsellers, including *Middle School, I Funny,* and *Jacky Ha-Ha,* and his books have sold more than 385 million copies worldwide. A tireless champion of the power of books and reading, Patterson created a children's book imprint, JIMMY Patterson Books, whose mission is simple: "We want every kid who finishes a JIMMY Book to say, 'PLEASE GIVE ME ANOTHER BOOK.'" He has donated more than three million books to students and soldiers and funds more than four hundred Teacher and Writer Education Scholarships at twenty-one colleges and universities. He has also donated millions of dollars to independent bookstores and school libraries. Patterson invests proceeds from the sales of JIMMY Patterson Books in pro-reading initiatives.

Chris Grabenstein is a *New York Times*–bestselling author who has collaborated with James Patterson on the I Funny, Jacky Ha-Ha, Treasure Hunters, House of Robots, and Max Einstein series, as well as *Word of Mouse, Katt vs. Dogg, Pottymouth and Stoopid, Laugh Out Loud,* and *Daniel X: Armageddon*. He lives in New York City.